Voices From
the Thai Countryside:

"The Necklace" and Other Stories
by Samruam Singh

Edited and Translated by
Katherine A. Bowie

University of Wisconsin
Center for Southeast Asian Studies
Monograph 17

Revised Edition: 1998

ISBN Cloth 1-881-261-24-7
ISBN Paper 1-881-261-25-5

Published by the Center for Southeast Asian Studies
University of Wisconsin-Madison
Madison, WI 53706 USA

Telephone: (608) 263-1755
Fax: (608) 263-3735

Illustrations by Jongrak Siritan
Front cover illustration by Jongrak Siritan

Designed by Cristina Rutter

To Yai, Yo, Jiew and Muk
in the hope that as you grow older
you will learn more about
the remarkable man your
father was.

Contents

Preface   *vii*

Note on Translation   *xi*

Transliteration   *xiii*

Part I: Introduction   *1*

The Historical Context of the 1970s in Thailand   *2*
> October 14, 1973 to October 6, 1976
> Changes Preceding 1973
> Changing Conditions for Urban Workers
> Changing Conditions for Peasants
> Formation of the Farmers Federation of Thailand (FFT)
> Growing Nationwide Polarization

Literature for Life   *10*
> Art for Life
> Surasingh's Commitment to Society

The Freedom of Fiction   *14*
> The Problem of Censorship: Cloaks of Fiction
> The Possibilities of New Journalism

The Art of Fiction   *17*
> Portrayal of Village Life
> The Artistry of Realism
> Strong, Resourceful Characters
> Characters Within a Social System
> Technique of Indirection
> Simplicity of Language
> Towards an Understanding of Social Issues
> Unsettling Conclusions

After the Stories   *22*

References   *33*

Part II: The Stories

A Curse on Your Paddyfields   41

Daughter for Sale.   *47*

Escaping the Middleman   *53*

Bitterness and the Sold Water Buffalo   *59*

Dividing the Rice   *65*

The Fount of Compassion   *71*

Burmese Buddha Images   *79*

Amphorn's New Hope   *85*

Khunthong's Tomorrow   *91*

Rit's First Mistake   *99*

Before Dawn   *109*

Kao Ying!   *119*

The Necklace   *125*

Glossary   *134*

Preface 1998

I first traveled to Thailand in the summer of 1974, less than a year after a massive popular uprising forced the military dictatorship of that country into exile. The new civilian government, headed by a highly respected university rector, had moved rapidly to lift censorship restrictions. It was a dramatic period. Seminars, debates, and a wide array of newspapers, books, and other publications flourished; over fifty political parties sprang into existence. Long-existent social problems such as prostitution, crime, drug addiction, malnutrition, poor medical care, Dickensian working conditions, and unemployment began to receive attention. Nonetheless, the threat of the return of military power was ever-present, casting a pall over the popular expression of grievances.

It was during these turbulent times that I arrived in Thailand, struggling to learn Thai and straining to understand the events surrounding me. Although a young graduate student in anthropology at the time, I decided to take a job as a research editor so that I could stay in Thailand longer. I also worked as a free-lance journalist, traveling to the various regions of the country in order to better familiarize myself with ongoing issues and events. I soon learned what every serious Thai journalist knew—that covering political events can be dangerous and even fatal. During this period, several journalists were assassinated and I received my first death threat. I decided that, however much the ongoing changes in Thai society intrigued me, it would be wise to avoid sensitive political subjects for my dissertation research. My interest in the contemporary issues, however, continued; the more I learned about village life, the more I wanted to find a way to communicate my experiences with others.

Translating these short stories seemed to be one way to share images of Thai village life with an English-speaking audience. Village life provoked in me a range of intense emotions. One of my earliest memories is of the outrage I felt at the off-duty policeman who got drunk at a village festival and emptied his gun into the crowd, wounding three people. I also remember with pain the young daughter of a village headman who committed suicide rather than let her parents sell their land so she could have surgery for her brain tumor; she had been worried that her younger siblings would not have much of a future were she to have surgery. I remember threshing rice with village friends at night, the grain golden in the glow of the kerosene lantern hanging nearby and everyone exuberant from singing, drinking rice-wine, sweating, and the knowledge that, for a time at least, there would be rice in their granaries. I remember with pride the little bamboo sleeping room villagers built for me; it was one of many times I witnessed the strength of intra-village cooperation. Surasingh's short stories resonated with and confirmed my experiences of the beauty and tragedy in Thai village life under rapidly changing circumstances.

My reason for translating these stories paralleled the author's own intentions. Surasinghsamruam Shimbhanao (the author's real name) wrote these stories to convey village events to a Thai urban audience, most of whom had never eaten or slept in a village. Using his literary skills and his profound knowledge of the countryside, Surasingh sought to convey vignettes of everyday village life. Although written in the 1970s, the struggles they describe remain current.

Knowing that so many people are enjoying reading these short stories is gratifying. Published in 1990, the first edition has already gone through several reprints. Although planned for some time, the timing of this new edition is poignant. Surasingh died of liver cancer on March 18, 1996.[1] His death was sudden and unexpected; he only learned he had cancer on January 25.[2] He was just 46 years old at the time. Although he had stopped writing short stories by the 1980s, his interest in literature and writing continued throughout his life, even during his years in Bangkok.

I had known Surasingh since 1976 when I first decided to conduct fieldwork in a northern Thai village. I had originally planned to live with the northern head of the Farmers Federation of Thailand; however, a bomb was thrown at his house and he went underground. The coup of October 6, 1976 made the climate for village research even more tense. During this period, Surasingh was a teacher at the Chiang Mai Teachers College. In addition to teaching Thai folklore and literature, he also oversaw the college's program for its students practice teaching in village elementary schools. Consequently he made use of his wide network of friends among school teachers and school principals to help me choose a village to conduct my own fieldwork. I eventually settled in a village in Sanpatong District, in Chiang Mai Province, only ten kilometers away from where Surasingh was then living.

Surasingh always kept an ear open for how I was doing. He taught me much about village life, from the fine points of etiquette such as how to eat sticky rice and how to walk quietly in wooden houses, to the intricacies of the meanings of their rituals. I was quite stunned by him. Despite his difficulty in those early days understanding spoken English, he had read widely in English. I had never expected to meet a Thai villager wanting to debate Levi-Strauss's structuralist approach to myth analysis. We became close friends, my knowledge of academic theories complementing his knowledge of village realities. Although both our lives changed dramatically over the course of the past two decades from those earlier village-based years, we always stayed in touch. My career owes much to his intellectual breadth, his political integrity, and his personal compassion.

This edition includes Surasingh's prize-winning short story, "The Neck-lace." This story was translated earlier into English by Ben Anderson and Ruchira Mendiones, both at Cornell University. However, as one of his most important short stories, it made sense to include it in this collection.[3] Since each translator's style varies, I decided to retranslate it in a manner consistent with the others in this volume. Furthermore, because Anderson did not consult with Surasingh, he misconstrues the author's position and the meaning of the story's last lines in his introduction to their important volume, *In the Mirror: Literature and Politics in Siam in the American Era.*

Anderson suggests that "The Necklace" needs to be read bifocally, "both as a glimpse of modern Hmong life and as an illustration of the difficult transition, even for progressive young Thai intellectuals, from ethnic self-absorption to political nationalism."[4] Anderson proposes that Surasingh's story, "for all its progressive coloration, is quite similar to that of the Thai state." He suggests that the hero and heroine of the story, "a few superficial folklorique details aside," "might well be Thai." Anderson bases his analysis primarily on the last lines of the story, disdaining the wife's use of Thai and the word "Meo" as "a derogatory Thai word for the Hmong."[5] Anderson suggests these lines reveal "the powerful, if unconscious, assimilationism of the writer's thought: Lao Jong and his wife appear less as Hmong than as Thai acting the parts of Hmong."[6]

Portraying *Lao* Jong and his wife as quasi-Thai was precisely Surasingh's point. While the prejudiced Thai reading audience at large may blame polygamy, opium cultivation, or other aspects of Hmong culture for their problems, Surasingh deliberately described the real life case of a Hmong couple who had made every effort to assimilate. Hmong traditionally practice "swidden" agriculture in which new mountain plots are cleared and cultivated for a time, and then left to return to nature. *Lao* Jong only had one wife; he shared work responsibilities with his wife; he had moved down into the lowlands to practice fixed agriculture.

Surasingh had considerable first-hand knowledge of Hmong culture. Unlike many Thai people who had little interest in Hmong culture, Surasingh enjoyed spending time in their villages (he also spent considerable time working in Karen villages). Ethnic terms change over time. While today many African-Americans object to being called "Blacks" or "Negroes," earlier generations did not. Hmong villagers in the 1970s (and even today) described themselves as "Meo." The term "Hmong" gained currency in the United States during the 1980s. The word "Meo" appears in Surasingh's text as part of a saying popular in central Thai urban culture. Surasingh deliberately closed his short story with *Lao* Jong's wife, *Ee* Moi, speaking in central Thai as a way of reminding the reader of the role of the central Thai government in the lives of the Hmong. In addition to their own language, Hmong living in northern Thailand are far more likely to speak northern Thai rather than the official language of the government, central Thai.

This revised edition of Surasingh's short stories provides me with an opportunity to set the record straight. Once I learned of his illness, translating this short story also provided a reason for my last visits with him. We both found it surreal, but reassuring. Surasingh and I had discussed all my other translations of his stories in detail. Although he was too ill to verify this last translation in the same way he had the other stories, he answered my most pressing questions. He died less than two weeks after my last visit with him; his lifelong concerns live on in these short stories and other facets of his life's work.

A Note on Sources

My friendship with Surasinghsamruam Shimbhanao,[7] the author of these short stories, began in 1976. The information I use in the introduction to describe Surasingh's life is based on numerous conversations and interviews with the author, his family and friends.

August 1998

Notes

[1] He actually died at 1:50 am on March 19, but in accordance with northern village traditions which surround the early morning hours with an ambiguity, his family prefers March 18. As his mother explained, "March 18 was a holy day (*wan phra*). He was also born on a holy day." I have chosen to abide by his mother's preference.

Liver cancer is more common in Southeast Asian than in many other parts of the world, primarily due to the increased incidence of hepatitis. Young men in their forties are its frequent victims. Surasingh never learned the factors behind his own case. His own father died at age 45 of liver disease.

[2] The surprise at the news of his death was noted in a column in the literary magazine *Cho Karaket* (March-April 1996; pp 23-24), edited by Suchart Sawatsri.

[3] This edition now includes all of Surasingh's short stories of which I am aware, with the exception of "Floating Rice" (*Khao Loi*) published in *Jaturat 2*, No. 50 (June 22, 1976): 42-43. Once I learned of Surasingh's illness, I prioritized translating "The Necklace." "Floating Rice" is written in an obviously pedantic style, as Surasingh's somewhat satirical response to criticism he had been receiving from fellow leftists for being overtly artistic and insufficiently didactic. Nonetheless it is interesting for its detailed description of the difficulties of growing rice.

[4] Benedict R. O'G. Anderson and Ruchira Meniones, eds. *In the Mirror: Literature and Politics in Siam in the American Era*. (Bangkok: Editions Duang Kamol, 1985), p. 76

[5] ibid., p. 81

[6] ibid., p. 82

[7] Shimbhanao is Surasingh's preferred spelling of his own name. Anderson (1983) transliterates the name as Chimpanao.

Note on Translation

The short stories in this collection were all written for the magazine *Jatu-rat*. The magazine was closed down by the government, however, before three of the stories were published. The unpublished Thai versions of these stories were made available to me by the author in 1978. The stories published in *Jat-urat* had to conform to the magazine's specifications of a length of two printed pages, with sufficient room left for illustrations. Consequently, the stories were written in a succinct style. After their publication, the author wrote other versions of the stories in which he expanded some sections of the text, particularly adding descriptive detail to help clarify the stories for urban or non–Thai audiences. In consultation with the author, only two of these additions have been retained, where they seemed necessary for understanding by Western readers. These additions have been footnoted. Otherwise, Surasingh preferred the translation to be of the published version of his stories, in order to reflect both the editorial and political constraints under which they were published.

There are numerous words in every source language that cannot be fully translated into a second language, given the unique social contexts that have infused the words with meaning. A particular example of this from Thai is the use of kinship terms as terms of address. Villagers address or refer to each other with various kinship terms according to the age of the speaker, the age and sex of the referent, and the nature of the emotional bond between them. For example, the term "*Yai*" can be translated as "grandmother." However, in "Daughter for Sale," *Yai* Phloy is not the father's grandmother, nor an old lady, but a mid-dle–aged woman slightly older than him, with whom he has no close relationship. I have made the decision to leave these kinship terms of address in Thai since there is no direct English translation with the numerous levels of meaning implied by the Thai term. Each term is explained in the glossary at the end of the volume.

At several stages of these translations, Surasingh and I discussed uncer-tainties and ambiguities in language and meaning, and he has read the final version of all except the last short story. I remain, however, responsible for the translation. Every translator faces the problem of gaining sufficient distance from the original text and language in order to present the translated text in an idiomatic form. I would like to express my appreciation to Jay Hill, John

Cadet, Chayan Vaddhanaphuti, David Streckfuss, Sarah Gardner, Carol Mitchell, Al Gunther, Bob Bickner, Dan Doeppers, Al McCoy, Nalinee Tantuvanit, Samart Srijumnong, Jongrak Siritan, and Trudi and Walter Bowie for their assistance with various phases of this work. I would also like to thank Vichien Kerdsuk, Megan Sinnott, Supeecha Baothip, Mark Desrosiers, and Cristina Rutter for their various roles in preparing this revised edition. Special thanks are due to Craig Reynolds, Joyce Burkhalter Flueckiger, and Hugh Wilson for their careful editorial readings of both the Introduction and the short stories. And, of course, I would like to acknowledge Surasingh for letting me translate his stories. I hope these translations will indeed provide opportunities for voices from the Thai countryside to be heard.

Katherine Bowie
August 1998

Transliteration

Thai may be transliterated in several ways. I have transliterated phonetically except in cases of proper names or words that have come to have a common English spelling, such as *baht* (which according to the system I am using would be transliterated as *baat*). In transliterating proper names, I have followed the spelling which has most frequently appeared in English before or have used the person's own preferred spelling.

A Guide to Pronunciation

Consonants	Pronounced like the
j	j in jam
k	g in good
kh	k in kitten
p	b in bad
ph	p in purse

Vowels	Pronounced like the
ai	ie in tie
ao	ow in cow
ae	a in mare
yy	i in bird
oh	aw in bawdy
aa	a in barn
ii	ee in see

Introduction

The short stories gathered in this collection are set in northern Thailand during the mid–1970s; they are brief episodes from the lives of ordinary villagers. The Buddha images, water buffaloes, Hmong hilltribes, lemon trees, market places, leaf–roofed village houses, tobacco–curing stations, and green paddyfields conform with stereotypical tourist images of the the northern region. These stories encourage the reader to penetrate beyond the physical beauty of the countryside, however, to a deeper understanding of village life. It is for this reason that as an anthropologist I became interested in translating the short stories of Samruam Singh.[1] Through these stories, numerous experiences of Thai villagers are given voice.

The stories in this collection provide insights into northern Thai village life and offer valuable testimony on a specific, dramatic period in Thai history. They were written in the wake of the popular uprising which had led to the ouster of the military government on October 14, 1973, inaugurating a brief civilian interlude. The three–year period of civilian rule was an exciting period of political, economic, social, and intellectual changes, many of which are described in the stories.

Surasinghsamruam Shimbhanao, or more simply Surasingh, was teaching literature at a teachers' college in northern Thailand and serving as a special correspondent for various Bangkok publications when he wrote these short stories. His position as a college teacher made him a government official. Consequently, he followed the Thai convention of using a pseudonym. He published his short stories under the pen name, Samruam Singh. The stories themselves were written specifically for publication in *Jaturat* [The Square], a respected weekly magazine that was abruptly closed down with the return of military rule in the bloody coup of October 6, 1976. Four short stories in this collection were not published in *Jaturat* since the magazine was closed down first.[2]

Journalistic constraints played an important role in Surasingh's decision to write short stories. In the course of his news reporting, he encountered events which, for a variety of reasons, he was unable to report in the traditional news story format. One reason was that newspapers were generally oriented to news–breaking events, and Surasingh wanted to include ongoing and everyday events in his writing. Further, Thai newspapers usually focussed on issues of interest to the nation's elite; Surasingh wanted to generate interest in the ordinary struggles of common villagers. Perhaps the most significant factor influencing his choice of the short story format was fear of political repercussions. Although these short stories were written during the more liberal period of civilian government, censorship remained an implicit threat. Influenced both by the Literature for Life movement occurring in Thailand and the New Journalism movement taking place in the United States, Surasingh molded the short story into a medium through which he could circumvent censorship and write about village life.

Surasingh had long been profoundly concerned with issues of social justice and, like many others of his generation, he had been subjected to government harassment for his views. His commitment to improving the condition of the poor and disadvantaged in Thai society had high personal costs—including the breakup of his marriage and forfeiture of his secure job as a college teacher. These short stories are a manifestation of Surasingh's engagement with the complexities of social change in Thai society. One of Thailand's few intellectuals to come from a village background, his knowledge of rural life was profound.[3] The stories are the result of his efforts to merge his knowledge of village social problems with his interests in journalism, literature, and education.

Surasingh won recognition both for his fiction and non–fiction writing. His book *Traditional Northern Thai Children's Play* was nominated for the National Book Award in 1977. He is considered one of Thailand's best short story writers. His short story "The Necklace" won the highly respected *Cho Karaket* Prize in 1979; and he was one of the thirteen authors whose works were chosen for translation in the collection of Benedict Anderson and Ruchira Mendiones (1985)[4] Many of his other published stories have enjoyed continuing popularity in Thailand, having been pirated and reprinted in various magazines. Much of Surasingh's success lies in his dual ability to bring literary skill to non–fiction and keen social observation to literary fiction.

In the pages that follow, I describe the historical, literary, and biographical context in which these short stories were written. In so doing, I show how Surasingh's short stories are significant for their literary style, for their insights into village life, and for their powerful commentary on the historical period in which they were written.

The Historical Context of the 1970's Thailand

October 14, 1973 to October 6, 1976.

The period of the mid–1970s—during which the short stories in this collection were written—was one of the most exciting periods in Thai history. Social change was occurring on an unprecedented scale. Until 1932, Thailand had been ruled by an absolute monarchy.[5] In that year a constitutional monarchy was established, and initially hopes were high that Thailand would institute a democratic form of government. However these hopes proved short–lived, as the brief rule of the civilian government was rapidly succeeded by a series of military regimes.

As the power of the military grew, particularly after World War II, discontent increased. Finally, growing popular unrest culminated with a mass uprising on October 14, 1973. The immediate cause of the uprising was the arrest on October 6, 1973 of thirteen university professors and students who had been distributing leaflets calling for a new constitution. The government announced that the police had discovered a communist plot to overthrow the administration and the thirteen were charged with treason. The public responded with widespread skepticism and anger.

On October 14, 1973 over 400,000 people marched to Democracy Monument in Bangkok. Military and riot police clashed with the demonstrators, and over 100 unarmed students and demonstrators were killed during the conflict (Morell and Samudavanija 1981:147; Keyes 1989:84). As marchers fled to the royal palace and elsewhere for safety, the King intervened and personally ordered the military triumvirate to leave the country on October 14, 1973, thereby ushering in a three–year period of civilian government (Morell and Samudavanija 1981:147).

During the three–year period of democratic government, students, workers, and farmers were free to express their opinions and grievances more freely than ever before. However, to some members of the Thai elite, this burst of political freedom was seen as opening Pandora's box. In addition, massive economic pressures, some beyond the ability of the civilian government to control and others the result of the previous policies of the military government, contributed to the growing political instability of the democratic government.

This brief, but exciting interregnum of civilian government was brought to a tragic end on October 6, 1976 by a bloody attack on Thammasat University in which scores of students were killed. A military coup followed a few hours later.[6] The brutal attack on the university is graphically summarized by David Morell and Chai–anan Samudavanija:

> As dawn broke over the city, . . . the time for any discussions had passed. By then, hundreds of armed policemen and several heavily armed Border Patrol Police units had joined the Village Scouts, Red Gaurs, and other vigilantes. As the mob tried to force its way through the locked gates of the campus, shooting broke out. Armed with M–16s, M–79 grenade launchers, carbines, and even recoilless rifles, the BPP [KAB: Border Patrol Police] and other armed individuals cut loose with a withering volume of fire. With police in the lead, the mob stormed the campus.

The carnage was almost unbelievable. Some students were burned alive or lynched from nearby trees; others were simply shot at point–blank range, some on the university grounds, others as they attempted to flee the campus on foot or swim to safety (Thammasat University is located on the bank of the Chao Phya River). Official government reports later listed forty–six dead, but other observers believe the toll was much higher. Hundreds were wounded. During and after the brutal slaughter some 1300 students at Thammasat were arrested and subsequently carted away in a convoy of buses, which were stoned by rightists (Morell and Samudavanija 1981:275).[7]

In the days following the bloody return of military rule, at least 3,000 people were arrested and thousands more fled underground. Many joined the growing ranks of the Communist Party of Thailand (CPT).

The majority of the stories in this collection were written and published during the three–year span of civilian government. During this period, numerous newspapers and magazines sprang into existence. Although censorship was still a factor, it was possible to write on more subjects than under the military rule which had preceded. After the 1976 coup, hundreds of these publications were closed down, and only those acceptable to the military government were allowed to continue.

Changes Preceding 1973

The brief civilian interlude in military rule explains the timing of the publication of these short stories. An explanation of the subject matter of Surasingh's short stories, however, is more complex and necessitates an understanding of the social changes occurring in Thai society both before and after 1973. In large part, these changes cannot be understood in isolation from international influences.

Before World War II, colonial powers, particularly the British, influenced the development of the Thai economy.[8] After World War II, U.S. involvement in Thailand became pronounced as an increasingly interventionist and actively anti–communist U.S. foreign policy took hold. After the Communist victory in China, the U.S. provided assistance for the development of the Thai police and military forces.[9] With the escalation of U.S. involvement in Vietnam during the 1960s, U.S. presence in Thailand expanded and became all–pervasive. One scholar describes the situation as follows:

By the late 1960s Thailand had much of the appearance of an occupied country. It was literally a garrison. The combined strength of Thai military and police forces, trained and equipped by the US (over 15,000 Thais received military or police officer training in the US and another 30,000 in Thailand) numbered around 260,000. Additionally there were some 50,000 US troops stationed there on seven major air bases (including one that could handle B–52 bombers), nine major strategic communications centres, six special forces headquarters and one naval base. From 1950–71, the US sent a total of over $600 million in economic and $950 million in military aid. There were US advisers everywhere; they occupied choice residences in the best districts of Bangkok (usually with four or five servants per household); sat in the highest positions in Thai government ministries and in the military; and were seen at the best golf and country clubs. In the towns where the military had bases, shantytowns sprouted, of bars, brothels, tailoring establishments, and off–base housing for the GI's to house Thai mistresses (Bell 1978:64).[10]

Together with growing U.S. military involvement, U.S. involvement in Thai government policymaking had major repercussions throughout Thai society. American advisors promoted private enterprise and foreign investment; they also encouraged the dismantling of state enterprises and helped to write new legislation granting highly preferential terms to foreign capital.[11] As a result, "foreign businessmen began to respond to the investment inducements of the Thai government, with Ford, Bristol–Myers, and Mercedes–Benz among the first of hundreds of multinational corporations that were eventually to open assembly plants in the kingdom" (Phillips 1987:6–7).

Changing Conditions for Urban Workers

These shifts in national economic priorities had important consequences for the daily lives of villagers. The 1960s saw extraordinarily rapid industrial expansion, particularly in the textile and food–processing industries. Growing numbers of villagers sought employment in factories and urban centers. From 1960 to 1970, the nonagricultural labor force increased by more than 1 million, from 2.12 million to 3.19 million. The relative size of the agricultural labor force declined from 83 percent of the country's total labor force in 1960 to 78 percent in 1970 (Morell and Samudavanija 1981:185). Laced throughout Surasingh's short stories are references to such villagers seeking nonagricultural employment.

Conditions for Thai workers were often Dickensian. Labor unrest escalated, brought about by a combination of new labor legislation, inflation, rice shortages, and other economic changes. The average number of strikes between 1966 and 1972 was less than twenty per year. Yet in 1973 alone there were 577 labor disputes; over 500 ended in strikes, with nearly 178,000 workers involved. Although the following two years saw a decline in the number of strikes, their average duration grew noticeably; the average number of work days lost per strike increased about three–fold (Morell and Samudavanija 1981:188).

Low wages were a major factor contributing to worker discontent. A Labor Department survey in 1972 found average *monthly* income for workers twenty to twenty–nine years of age was about 480 baht ($24.00); for workers thirty to thirty–nine years old, the average income was about 830 baht ($41.50) (Morell and Samudavanija 1981:194).[12] In 1973 a minimum wage law went into effect, setting the minimum wage at twelve baht a day (sixty cents); however, this wage law only applied to the capital city of Bangkok and the immediately adjacent provinces. Not until October 1974 was a countrywide wage established for the first time: ten baht a day (fifty cents).

The institution of a minimum wage did little to improve the condition of the workers. As Morell and Samudavanija explain, "Real wages were already at about this level, and the rate of inflation was such that purchasing power among low–income groups was almost halved."[13] Before 1973 the increase in the cost of living had been about 1.5 to 2 percent per year; in 1973–74 prices rose an average of 5 percent per month (Morell and Samudavanija 1981:194). Nor were the minimum wage laws or any other labor protection laws passed by the civilian government actively enforced.[14] Given such oppressive conditions, it is not surprising that Thai workers sought redress of their grievances. However, only a minority of workers were able to organize for improved conditions. Workers employed in small factories, particularly those located away from the capital center, were rarely unionized.

Changing Conditions for Peasants

While several of Surasingh's short stories portray the plight of villagers working in factories, the majority of his stories concern events occurring in the countryside. The agrarian sector is by far the dominant sector of Thai society. In 1970, 78 percent of Thailand's population lived in villages, engaged predominantly in rice agriculture (Turton 1978:106).[15] Agricultural products accounted for over half of all exports by value. Despite agriculture's economic importance, however, the military government paid little attention to its improvement. Thus, long–standing problems of poverty, landlessness, and indebtedness continued unabated and even worsened.

During the 1960s the number of villagers living below the officially defined poverty line increased. In 1963 the average farm size in northern Thailand was 16.1 *rai*; by 1973 this figure had dropped to 8.8 *rai*. Ten *rai* (four acres) is considered the minimum land area necessary for subsistence (Turton 1978:111). By 1971, 63 percent of northern and 74 percent of northeastern rural households were living in poverty (Turton 1978:108). Further, land ownership was not, and still is not, equally distributed. According to the Land Development Department, 48 percent of Thailand's 5.5 million agricultural households own 16 percent of cultivated land (Turton 1978:111). The extent of agrarian poverty was and remains even greater than mere figures on landholding patterns suggest, since landless villagers—both tenants and wage workers—are not included in land ownership surveys.

In some cases, landless villagers were able to work land as tenants. Tenancy was highest in the central and northern regions of Thailand; in some districts in the central plains area tenancy was as high as 90 percent (Turton 1978:113). In the northern region, where all of these short stories are set, the highest quality irrigated paddylands were often owned by absentee landlords and worked by local tenants; landlords often took as much as two–thirds of the harvested crop as rent.

Figures on the numbers of landless agricultural workers are difficult to obtain. One district survey taken in 1974 in the northern province of Chiang Mai 1974 found 36 percent of households were completely landless (Turton 1978:112). My own research in another district of this same northern province corroborates this figure. These landless villagers worked as hired laborers whenever possible. At other times of the year they caught fish, collected bamboo shoots, mushrooms, or other forest products; some villagers were reduced to begging.

Another important component of rural economic distress was indebtedness. A 1968 survey conducted by the National Statistical Office reported that 4 million out of 5 million farming families were in debt. The average farm family's debt was about $200, as compared to an average family income of not more than $300 a year; some families earned as little as $25 a year (Morell and Samudavanija 1981:209). Only 10–15 percent of all credit was provided through official government or bank sources (Turton 1978:116). While the legal interest rate was 10–14 percent per *year,* the more readily available unofficial local rates were 5–10 percent per *month.* Thus, once a villager was forced to borrow money at private rates, he had little hope for escape from his indebtedness.

Surasingh's short stories are set against this background of rural dislocation and change. The characters in his stories range from the daughter of a wealthy village family to tenants and landless peasants. The theme of indebtedness runs through many of the stories, sometimes as a consequence of illness or other unavoidable needs, and sometimes because a character took a risk to improve his family's situation.

Formation of the Farmers Federation of Thailand (FFT)

The importance of the growing economic problems of the countryside became clearer during the mid–1970s, as peasants began to agitate politically. The effects of previous government policy, together with growing land pressure, mounting indebtedness, and declining real wages, were taking their toll.

In May 1974 hundreds of farmers demonstrated to protest the dispossession of their land by moneylenders. In response, the civilian Prime Minister established a national committee to investigate their grievances. In its first month of operation (June 1974), the committee received an astonishing 10,999 petitions from farmers. By the end of September 1974, the committee had received 53,650 formal petitions (Morell and Samudavanija 1981:216). In addition to petitions, farmers began to draw attention to their problems by demonstrating. From June 24–29, 1974 thousands of farmers gathered in the capital.[16] In November 1974 some 1,200 farmers representing twenty–five provinces in the North, Northeast and Central areas met in Bangkok. Simultaneously, there were eighteen days of continuous meetings in Chiang Mai, the largest city of the north. The Chiang Mai meeting sent representatives to Bangkok. The result was the formation of the historic Farmers' Federation of Thailand (FFT) on November 19, 1974.[17] The FFT's activities grew rapidly, especially in the north, where the rate of tenancy was particularly high.

The growing popular pressure resulted in the newly formed Parliament passing the Agricultural Land Rent Control Act on December 6, 1974 (Morell and Samudavanija 1981:221). This act was aimed primarily at easing the plight of tenants, requiring a contract for all tenancies for six–year periods and limiting the maximum rent to one–third of the crop. The Land Rent Control Act was followed by the passage of the Agricultural Land Reform Act in January 1975, meant to come into force January 1, 1977. This act set a maximum ceiling on landholdings at fifty *rai*.[18]

The principal activity of the FFT was to make known the provisions of the new acts and to support those farmers who pressed for their implementation. As the FFT continued to grow, even publishing its own newspaper, tension began to intensify. Since the FFT was the farmers' own independent organization and not subject to government regulations, government officials accused the FFT of being illegal (Morell and Samudavanija 1981:224). The FFT's efforts to hold village meetings to inform villagers of their new rights under the laws were branded as the work of communists "agitating the masses." FFT meetings were harassed and attacked by the police and military as well as private right–wing groups.[19]

A wave of assassinations began, with twenty–one FFT leaders murdered between March and August 1975 (Morell and Samudavanija 1981:225).[20] No arrests were ever made in this wave of murders. As Morell and Samudavanija write:

> These murders seem to have been part of an organized plan of political intimidation. Almost all of those murdered were active FFT members. All the killings took place within a relatively short period of time and then suddenly stopped. In many cases the assassins' actions were highly professional, not characteristic of the behavior of an ordinary villager, no matter how angry or full of revenge. The killers seem to have been hired for this job, and none of the assassins was ever caught by the police. Some suspected that *Nawaphon*[21] was responsible for

at least some of these killings ... A number of students, among others, alleged that members of the army's hunter–killer teams or the Border Patrol Police were the professional hit men for these killings, acting under contract to Nawaphon, local officials, or local land owners (1981:225).

Although all of Surasingh's short stories were written in the context of these heightening rural tensions, they usually deal with village political mobilization only indirectly. His intention is to facilitate the reader's understanding of the vast changes taking place in rural society. In the story "Dividing the Rice," Surasingh reveals most directly his characteristically complex view of village discussions of the FFT and the Land Reform Act. Rather than making a facile advocacy of this Act, he describes the ways in which landholding villagers came to own land and is sensitive to the web of relations that bind landowning and landless villagers together.

Growing Nationwide Polarization

As a result of these dramatic social, economic, and political upheavals in Thai society, there was a growing polarization on the political spectrum. Peaceful legal movements for social reform included a wide range of liberal and leftist political parties; in addition there was a growing communist insurgency. On the right, a variety of new organizations emerged, principal among them the Red Gaurs, Nawaphon, and the Village Scouts. All three were supported by leading members of the military and police elite and prominent businessmen. Like the unprecedented movements on the Left, the rightist mobilization was also a new development in Thai history. Both were seeking "the hearts and minds" of the population, with the Right couching its ideological appeals in terms of the symbols of "King, Nation, and Religion."

During the 1970s, political violence increased dramatically.[22] The growing right–wing movement was a response to the demands for change throughout the country and a growing insurgency (see Bowie 1997). In addition to the leaders of the farmer's movement, union organizers, students leaders, and other political activists were also targeted for assassination. In March 1976, Dr. Boonsanong Punyodyana, the Secretary–General of the Socialist Party of Thailand, was assassinated near his home. On March 20–21, 1976, at demonstrations demanding the withdrawal of American troops from Thailand (which numbered some 30,000), grenades and plastic bombs were thrown into the crowd: four people were killed and eighty–five injured (Morell and Samudavanija 1981:167).

The elections of April 1976 were the bloodiest in Thai history. Over thirty people were killed during the election campaign, and dozens more were injured in various incidents.[23] The battle for the "hearts and minds" of the people was escalating. In addition to outright violence and physical intimidation, rightist efforts to control popular attitudes took a variety of more subtle forms. New religious groups such as Pu–Suwan Institute arose, which distributed amulets to soldiers to protect them in their battles with communists, and which claimed the Buddha had ordered them to lead a movement to save Thai society from communism. Seances were also held in which the institute's director communicated with the spirits of Gandhi, Karl Marx, and prominent Thai ghosts, all of whom were said to be advising the institute (Morell and Samudavanija 1981:248).

In addition, the government radio stations and local newspapers disseminated a variety of anti–communist programs, encouraging superstitions and manipulating village beliefs.[24] For example, in order to accentuate ethnic divisions in the northeast, rumors were started that Vietnamese food caused penises to shrink. In an effort to control the student movement and make it difficult for students to enter villages, rumors of *phiidutlyat* (blood–sucking vampires) were spread. These vampires were said to be dressed in farmer indigo–dyed shirts, with glasses, shoulder bags, and flip–flop sandals—characteristic symbols of the progressive students. Surasingh's short story "Before Dawn" is about the result of such government efforts to manipulate popular superstitions.

A knowledge of the historical context of Surasingh's short stories is important for an understanding of their content. The changing economic conditions of Thai workers and villagers described above are the fabric from which the plots of these stories are woven; the political mobilization of peasants, workers, and students is part of the inspiration behind many of the stories. The increased freedom of expression allowed by the democratic government of 1973–1976 enabled them to be published.

Literature For Life

Art for Life

The period of civilian government in the 1970s was a time of unprecedented literary creativity in Thailand, accompanied by lively critical discussion about the purpose of art and the role of intellectuals in society. Much of this discussion was similar to literary debates which had taken place among the European Left. However, Thailand also had its own tradition of critical thinkers.[25] Jit Phumisak's 1957 book, *Art for Life, Art for People*, became the lightning rod of controversy for the renewed discussion taking place in Thailand in the 1970s.[26] As Jit wrote, "There is no art that was not invented to serve a certain class. There is no art for art's sake; there is only art for serving a certain way of life" (1974:57–58).[27] He argued that the intrinsic social value of art was not measured by its popularity, but rather by its social effect:

Art that makes people dream of nonsense and leaves them concerned only with their own happiness despite the suffering of the rest
of the world or that makes people forget their social consciousness
and at the same time does not show men how to be creative or does
not inspire people to have critical minds to develop their own thoughts
is not "art for people". It is rather "art to intoxicate people"; art that
makes people think, however, about their real lives and understand
empirical reality, leads people to create their class consciousness which
is the symbol of certainty and inspires people to develop their
lives—that is "true art for people" . . . art for people aims at serving
people in fighting the evil in life to create a better life (translated in
Wedel and Wedel 1987:83).

In the wake of October 14, students, lecturers, writers, and other activists
began to debate the meaning of the work of Jit Phumisak and other important writers of the 1950s. Chonthira Kladyu's 1974 book, *People's Literature*
(*Wannakhadi khong Puangchon*), further popularized Jit's views and the question about the role of art and literature. The result was a surge in critical
discussion among Thai artists and scholars of all kinds.[28] One of the most
famous and successful expressions of these views on the role of art was given
by the musical group "Caravan," whose songs introduced the musical genre
"Music for Life" (*Dontrii phya Chiwit*).[29] Even though Caravan's songs were
banned in Thailand after 1976, the group's music continued to be popular, and
their musical and lyrical innovations continue to influence popular music in
Thailand today.

The movement to critically reevaluate Thai literature in the context of its
social relevance reached its most extreme pitch at a conference held at Chiang
Mai University in 1975 entitled "Should We Burn Thai Literature?"
(Poolthupya 1981:210). Although few scholars were in favor of such a drastic
measure, there was a growing consciousness of the relationship between literature and society. To the extent that much classical Thai literature was
court–oriented, scholars began to pay closer attention to the political content
and context of these texts. The reevaluation not only of contemporary writing, but also ancient classical works, indicates how widespread the concern for
social relevance was becoming.[30]

Surasingh, as all writers of this period, was aware of the controversies surrounding the relationship between literature and society. In addition to writing,
he also was teaching Thai language and literature. Therefore, his interest in
the subject was two–fold: while he held a deep appreciation for many of the
Thai classics, he also shared a sympathy for understanding art in its historical
and political context and was sympathetic to the creation of socially relevant
art.[31] He was interested in motivating people to become more involved in the
society around them and felt a special obligation to help improve the living conditions of villagers.[32]

Surasingh's Commitment to Society

In large measure, Surasingh's social commitment resulted from the difficulties and advantages of his own background. He was born in 1949 in
Thonburi, a city adjacent to Bangkok. However, his mother was from a village in the northern province of Lampang. Like many girls from poorer village
households, she had moved to Bangkok to work as a servant in the home of
wealthy distant relatives. During this time she met Surasingh's father, a north-
easterner who had come to Bangkok to study medicine.

Unfortunately, Surasingh's father's education was interrupted by the out-
break of World War II and by the fact that he now had a family to support.
Nonetheless, during his study, he had been able to acquire some basic famil-
iarity with Western medicine. After a few years in Bangkok, he and his wife
returned to his wife's village (the usual residence pattern for Thai villagers).
Surasingh was four or five years old at the time. His father began working as
local medic, and his mother sold homemade desserts in the village market.

Surasingh was among a small number of villagers of his generation who
received an advanced education. His awareness of the many obstacles placed
before village children seeking an education comes through clearly in the story
"Amphorn's Hope."Although he attended one of the best private schools in
Lampang province, his own course of study was not smooth. Surasingh's educational expenses were considerably reduced since he lived in a village near the
town of Lampang. Although his parents owned no land, their combined income
and assistance from relatives helped to make his education possible.

While pleased to be getting a good education, Surasingh knew he was not
like the other children attending the same school; they were city children from
wealthy families, whose parents would be able to buy or obtain through con-
nections high–paying jobs for them, whether or not they did well in school.
While they were being chauffeured to school every morning, Surasingh sold
flowers in the town market to defray his living expenses. The gap in the lifestyle
between rich and poor was thus concretely manifest to him at an early age.

Surasingh received teacher training certification and worked first as an assistant headmaster at a private school in Sanpatong District, Chiang Mai province.
He then became a rural elementary schoolteacher in the government public education system. Because of benefits afforded to government officials, he was
eligible for salary continuation while furthering his education. Thus Surasingh
returned to school, completing his B.A. in Education at Chiang Mai University in 1973. Among the thousands of candidates who took the national civil
service exam that year, Surasingh placed second in the nation, qualifying for a
position as a college teacher in the Department of Teacher Training, Ministry
of Education. Surasingh then taught in the southern teacher training college
of Nakhon Sri Thammarat, where he was awarded a double promotion for outstanding work. In 1975 he transferred back north to teach at Chiang Mai
Teachers College.

For Surasingh, teaching in the teacher training colleges was part of his social commitment.[33] Unlike the universities where ninety–four percent of the students are from urban backgrounds, the teacher training colleges are attended by primarily rural students (Girling 1981:89). These students generally graduate to become elementary schoolteachers in local village schools. Surasingh cared deeply about improving the quality of the rural educational system, particularly after his own experience as a village schoolteacher. In addition to his other duties, he supervised student teachers practicing in rural elementary schools.

As part of his effort to foster his students' pride in their rural heritage, Surasingh was instrumental in helping to establish the Lannathai Cultural Center at the Chiang Mai Teachers College; his students contributed many of the village artifacts still displayed at the Center. Surasingh also pursued research interests in village cultural beliefs and practices. He studied village folklore, jokes, old courtship poetry, spirit beliefs, religious rituals, folksongs, musical instruments, and children's games, publishing several academic articles on these subjects. He also encouraged his students to collect such information. In 1977 he published a book entitled *Traditional Northern Thai Children's Games (Kaanlalen khong dek lannathai)*, which was nominated for the National Book Award.

Surasingh kept abreast of village affairs by continuing to live in a village even when he was teaching in the town of Chiang Mai. As a result of his personal background, his supervision of students primarily from rural backgrounds, and his research interests, Surasingh was intimately familiar with a wide range of village issues. He was concerned about the changes he saw in the countryside around him and was committed to doing as much as possible to contribute to finding solutions to the problems of village life.

Teaching was one expression of Surasingh's social concern; writing was another. Already while he was in college, Surasingh had written a number of poems which were published in local magazines; he had also written various articles on village issues ranging from health care to education. While teaching at a teachers college in the south, Surasingh served as a member of the editorial board of the college's daily newspaper. Using a variety of pseudonyms, he was also a regular contributor of news articles and in–depth commentaries to the national level newspaper *Prachathipathai* and the well–known progressive magazine *Chaobaan*.[34] After Surasingh returned to Chiang Mai in 1975, he was asked to become the northern correspondent for *Jaturat* magazine. Surasingh agreed and began writing news articles on a regular basis for this magazine.

Jaturat was one of the most influential and respected periodicals of the civilian period.[35] Its editor, Pansak Vinyaratn, was a brilliant social analyst later serving as one of five advisors to the Prime Minister of Thailand, Chartchai Choonhavan, until that government was toppled by a military coup in February 1991. Pansak assembled an impressive editorial staff from among Thailand's intellectuals and writers. Key contributors included journalists and short story writers Khamsingh Srinawk and Suchart Sawatsri; the Buddhist intellectual

Sulak Sivaraksa was among those who served as an adviser.[36] All of the members of the editorial board were already well–known writers, scholars, and social critics. They were open to alternative formats for presenting the news and critical discussions of issues of social importance.

Most of Surasingh's contributions to *Jaturat* were either unsigned or written under pseudonyms. Signed articles included an account of a police raid on the Teachers College of Chiang Mai, the struggle of tobacco growers, and the problems of cattle–raisers. Other pieces were more analytical discussions of socio–economic problems and trends. Surasingh's writings reflect the unusual position and social commitment of their author, at once a villager and an educator. In his teaching, he was introducing primarily rural students to essentially urban literary traditions; in his writing, he was, in effect, teaching urban readers about village life.

The Freedom of Fiction

The Problem of Censorship: Cloaks of Fiction

However much Surasingh and other writers of his time felt a commitment to producing socially responsible writing, censorship remained a serious constraint. While the civilian period of 1975–1976 made the expression of a greater variety of opinions possible, the military remained a powerful, ever–present threat. He used the genre of short story as an innovative solution to the specific set of problems facing him as a journalist. His stories were written not primarily as works of creative literary fiction, but as veiled journalism.

Surasingh's return to the north from Bangkok in 1975 coincided with the period of growing activity by peasant leaders who were soon to form the Farmers Federation of Thailand and with a growing activism by students in both the teachers colleges and universities in the north. In the course of reporting developments in the north for *Jaturat,* Surasingh came across numerous dramatic incidents which were politically difficult to report. He had reason to fear for his own safety were he to report these incidents as news, since Thai journalists frequently had been subject to arrest, harassment, and even assassination.[37] Even though he did not sign—even with his pseudonym—many of his news stories, the fact that he was the primary northern correspondent for *Jaturat* would cast suspicion on him for any stories about events in the north. Furthermore, some incidents which villagers reported to him could have invited government harassment upon the villagers themselves. In other cases, the editors had reasons to fear that failure to practice self–censorship would hasten the likelihood of the publication being closed down.

Censorship in Thailand has taken many forms imposed with varying degrees of subtlety. In 1957 the military government issued Proclamation 17, which set the prevailing tone for the decades that followed. Broadly worded, it gave the government authority to seize and destroy any materials critical of the monarchy, the Thai government, or the Thai people, as well as any matter "tending to lower national morals or culture" (Phillips 1987:24–25).

Throughout the civilian interregnum, writers were conscious of the possibility that they or their publications could fall victim to varying forms of harassment, some involving direct applications of government authority and others involving extra–legal attacks. More subtle forms of harassment included:

> . . . "visits of inquiry" from the police . . . "words of warning" from an unknown official that are passed through a series of intermediaries; or anonymous letters or phone calls, phrased so they are taken seriously (Phillips 1987:25).

Thai writers devised a variety of stratagems to circumvent the constraints of censorship, such as:

> . . . underground publication; the use of a multiplicity of pseudonyms by certain authors (since frequently authors as well as texts are considered dangerous by censors); and the creative use of humor, hyperbole, and little symbolic conceits that, while brilliantly integrated into the text, make unmistakable political points (Phillips 1987:23).

Allegory, satire, and various forms of fiction also have been useful devices to avoid direct confrontations. Yuangrat Wedel has commented, "The device of using fiction . . . was particularly useful during times of government repression. Political tracts would be seized and burned while novels remained on sale" (Wedel and Wedel 1987:86).

For Surasingh, the short story genre provided one solution to his difficulty in reporting sensitive "news," enabling him to relate true events in the form of "fiction." Indeed, all the short stories in this collection are based on true incidents, including the stories "Dividing the Rice," "Before Dawn," "Burmese Buddha Images," and most particularly "Kao Ying," in which villagers end up killing a group of policemen. The short story format protected both the writer and the villagers involved, while allowing the incidents to be described.

Prior to the volatile context of the mid–1970s, Thailand already had a short story literary tradition overladen with political connotations, with which Surasingh was well acquainted. "Sanuk Nyk," written in 1886 by Prince Phichitprichakorn, is considered to have been Thailand's first short story and simultaneously Thailand's first piece of "formal realist" prose, fictional prose put in a realistic setting.[38] Its publication in *Wachirayan Wiset*, a bi–weekly journal of literary, social, and political criticism, created an uproar among conservative members of the court and infuriated the abbot of Wat Boworniwet, one of the most important temples in the country.[39]

The Possibilities of "New Journalism"

Political factors were not the only reason Surasingh found the short story to be a relevant medium for his ideas. Subject matter was a second important reason. Some of the events which Surasingh found powerfully compelling were small incidents he observed in the lives of villagers he met or knew personally. The everyday life of villagers—their resilience, resourcefulness, and pain in the face of daily events—impressed him, and he sought a way to record it. Yet according to the canons of traditional journalism, these everyday occurrences, however powerful, however painful and moving, were not "news." So Surasingh looked for an alternative literary form.[40]

In the course of his weekly readings of such international magazines as *Newsweek* and *Time,* Surasingh kept current with new literary directions in other countries. During the 1960s, there were important new developments in writing in the United States, many in response to the changing times and intensified upheavals of the opposition to the Vietnam War. Among these emergent literary forms was an innovative approach to journalism. Surasingh read or was aware of writers such as Truman Capote, Tom Wolf, and Norman Mailer. Their experiments with new styles of writing non–fiction allowed for a broad array of subject matter and became known as "New Journalism." New Journalists crossed traditional boundaries of appropriate subject matter, interviewing and focussing on "ordinary" people instead of limiting their reporting to "new" information and extraordinary events. As one commentator noted, they "looked into the lives of so–called ordinary individuals who seemed to typify a class or a group of people" (Mencher 1977:440).

Traditional journalism had also encouraged its reporters to record "just the facts." A good journalist was to be objective and nonpartisan. Any effort to describe how a participant in an event was feeling was decried as being subjective. New Journalists insisted that subjective sentiments of participants are as much a part of a "story" as who, what, when, and where. To the charge of partisanship, New Journalists responded that no news reporting was truly and wholly objective. They pointed to the numerous ways in which bias enters a news story, ranging from the choice of topic to choice of verbs.[41]

The New Journalists sought to engage the reader in a personal way by recreating the thoughts and feelings of people involved in the news story. They borrowed literary techniques from novelists and other fiction writers in their efforts to attain this immediacy and realism.[42] Communicating the human, existential reality was more important than mere technical accuracy. Thus, with New Journalism, the boundaries between fiction and non–fiction, never very clear, grew even more blurred.[43]

Surasingh's fiction resonates with the ideas of New Journalism.[44] Traditional journalism had not given him the freedom to write about what he felt was important. Listening to the debates on New Journalism, Surasingh found encouragement to experiment and created his own solution: through the use of the short story, he found a way to report events in the daily life of common people. He was interested in these events as they typified general trends in broader society and the characters which peopled them as typifying various social classes. He combined his ethical commitment to bring the experiences of ordinary villagers to life with his literary talents and keen empirical observations. Thus, Surasingh can be said to be one of Thailand's first "New Journalists."

The Art of Fiction

Realism in the Portrayal of Village Life

Surasingh's short stories, although originally published individually, gain strength and interest when read as a collection. For many urban Thai writers, rural life is populated by anonymous, homogenous villagers, passive victims of the social changes occurring around them. Through Surasingh's fiction, villagers come alive in all their rich diversity. In addition to the commonplace image of villagers as peasants with small plots of paddyland, Surasingh's stories include characters who are factory workers, hired workers in tobacco–curing stations, contractors, carpenters, construction workers, teachers, police, craftspeople, middlemen, market women, water–buffalo keepers, fishermen, hillpeople, and landless villagers. There is an intertextuality between stories that creates a sense that several of the stories may be referring to people in the same village. Read together, the stories create a rich collage of the diversity of village life, showing the innovative ways in which villagers seek their livelihood.

Surasingh's knowledge of village life is apparent in his accurate, detailed descriptions of characters, settings, and events. His accounts of tobacco–leaf sorting, fishing techniques, interest rates, crop prices, market organization, factory management, or the culture of the Hmong tribal peoples convey a sense of the rich array of skills and knowledge which villagers share. To recreate episodes from the lives of villagers realistically, Surasingh relied heavily on reconstructing conversations and events which he himself had witnessed in the countryside. Thus, his short stories give voice to villagers whose words had rarely been heard.

Unlike many others who have written on the peasantry in the highly politicized context of Thailand, Surasingh's short stories have little sentimentality. They are told simply; they are carefully structured and deliberately worded. Like Tolstoy and other realist writers, his art is in seeking to find words to describe reality without nostalgia or pedantry. Even when describing real events, Surasingh uses literary license to understate rather than to exaggerate misery or poverty. For example, in the story "Before Dawn" in which a villager is killed as a suspected *phiidutlyat* (blood–sucking ghost), Surasingh portrays the victim as someone who has escaped from the mental hospital. In fact, the individual killed in this particular incident was an ordinary villager, but Surasingh believed that this truth was too harsh, would evoke too much emotion, and the reader would reject it.[45] Surasingh used his art to "soften" events such as the murdered villager in order to force his readers to come to grips intellectually with the realities of Thai society.[46]

Strong, Resourceful Characters

Thai urban intellectuals often portray villagers as passive, pathetic peasants. In contrast, the villagers in Surasingh's fiction are deliberately never the poorest, weakest, or most tragic members of Thai society; rather they are generally resourceful, hard–working individuals. In "Amphorn's New Hope," the girl aspiring for an education is the daughter of a carpenter earning fifty baht a day, at a time when agricultural workers were earning fifteen baht a day. When some of the tenants in "Dividing the Rice" laugh at the impoverished fisherman,[47] they are reprimanded; one of the characters says, "It's not right to make fun of people worse off than ourselves."

Similarly, in "Khunthong's Tomorrow," the lead character is a teenage girl from the northeast, working under extremely poor conditions from 5 a.m. to 10 p.m. in a knitting factory. She and forty other girls eat and sleep in the same room in which they work. She complains of aching "from the tips of her fingers, her arms, her shoulders, all the way down to the small of her back." And yet the author takes pains to have Khunthong say to another new girl:

> Even though knitting may seem hard, it's still only indoor work. It's more comfortable than collecting clams, or crabs, or digging for crickets and *kutcii*, or gathering bamboo shoots or other plants. Before one has found enough to eat, just for one meal, the sun has burnt one's skin black.

Surasingh's characters each fight to do the best they can for themselves and their families. They are not, however, necessarily "virtuous" figures: they include an opium grower, a antique smuggler, a father who sells his daughter into prostitution, and a village youth who tears down election posters and creates disturbances at the events organized by opposing candidates. Nonetheless, the reader comes to identify with these characters who have been forced to make difficult and painful decisions in circumstances outside of their control.

Characters Within a Social System

By deliberately placing most of his characters in the middle of a broad social spectrum, with others both above and below them, Surasingh fulfilled several goals. First, realizing the character's position in relation to others raises the reader's awareness of the wider society. Second, the relative good fortune of the main character forces the reader to engage the character's conditions in a thoughtful way, eschewing mere pity. Surasingh uses the hope his characters have for the future as a way of challenging the reader, as well, to think about the future. When the character's hope in a given story has been dashed, the reader has been provided with enough understanding of the overall situation to contemplate the outcome had the character made different decisions. Surasingh wants the reader to be able to identify with the main characters and their plights, which would not be possible if they were too pathetic.[48]

Just as Surasingh's protagonists are complex, real figures, so are his antagonists; he refuses to allow the reader any easy answers, any easy targets for anger or frustration. The complexity of his fictional work is made even clearer by reading Surasingh's short stories in a collection. In the "Sold Water Buffalo," the enemies are the middlemen; in "Escaping the Middleman," one key character is herself a middleman. In "Daughter for Sale," the woman who is the go–between in recruiting prostitutes was herself once a prostitute, very likely sold by her parents. In this story, there is a painful irony in the fate of the children of the creditor and the debtor; the creditor wants the money to send his son overseas to study, but his demand for repayment results in the debtor selling his daughter. In "Dividing the Rice," the tenant's enemies are the landowners; yet Surasingh notes that, given the current crop prices, the landowners appeared to be doing tenants a favor by letting them rent—even at exorbitant rates—since they could have earned more money by selling the land and using that money to loan out with interest.

In "A Curse on Your Paddyfield," the reader identifies with the excitement of a landless fisherman using a new lantern for fishing. Surasingh takes pains to let the reader know that the fisherman had "carefully waded between the rows of planted ricestalks, looking right and left, concerned not to injure any of the seedlings." When the landowner's gun rings out, shattering the fisherman's lantern and his hopes, the reader cannot help but feel anger. However, rather than to leave the reader angry at the landowner, Surasingh insists on bringing the reader to a higher level of understanding by making the antagonist sympathetic as well. He writes:

> From the distance, he heard a voice yelling out after him, "You cur. Trampling everything down. So it's you who have been ruining the rice. Now I'll have to replant it all over again. I don't even have enough money to buy more seedlings.

The problems which Surasingh portrays in these short stories are not caused by individual characters; nor are the solutions to be found in individual characters making different decisions. By presenting both the protagonists and antagonists as sympathetic, Surasingh expands the reader's focus to the broader social context. The stories dramatize, in miniature, more complex issues in Thai society.

Technique of Indirection

Often the lead characters in Surasingh's stories are not the central actors in the narrated events, but are supporting actors. Surasingh relates many of his stories indirectly, thereby softening the reality of the narrated event. For example, the story of prostitution centers on the father and mother rather than the daughter being sold into prostitution. The love between the father and mother contrasts poignantly with the sexual liaisons the daughter will be forced to make; the mother asks, "I wonder how many husbands she will have had." Because the story's focus is not limited to the daughter's experience, the reader is encouraged to transcend narrow conclusions about gender and prostitution and engage instead the issues of social and class structure.

"Rit's First Mistake" is a story highlighting the situation of workers in Thailand. Rather than tell the story from the perspective of the injured construction worker, Surasingh tells the story through the eyes of the character Rit, who initially stands outside of the circle of laborers. (During a recent election, Rit had worked as a hired hoodlum for one of the political candidates.) The conclusion challenges the reader to ask whether Rit has made a mistake or essentially done the right thing by taking the side of the worker instead of the dishonest contractor.

Simplicity of Language

The artistry of Surasingh's writing style lies in its deceptive simplicity. Using as few superfluous words as possible—he was under severe word limitations owing to editorial restrictions writing for *Jaturat*—Surasingh sparsely outlines his key figures and events. He creates moods and establishes settings with a careful choice of adjectives and descriptive passages. In the opening scene of "Burmese Buddha Images," a story about smuggled antiquities, an old woman is chewing betel. Her betel set is carefully described. In the old days, betel sets were among the prize possessions and indicators of status of every household; thus, the betel set is an effective symbol of cherished antiquities. In "Kao Ying," the wasp becomes a small, powerful symbolic image of the story's theme. The story opens with children playing a game with two wasps clasped in battle. Surasingh explains that although now these wasps had become playthings to the children, they were in fact powerful insects if provoked: "The poison of one sting is sufficient to stupefy a grown man and, if attacked by swarms, even elephants succumb." The anecdote foreshadows the narrative. When one wasp is victorious, one of the children cries, "Kao Ying!" or "Victory!" At the end of the story, that cry recurs in another context, transfigured. The Hmong villagers cry "Kao Ying!" when they succeed in their struggle against the Thai policemen. Thus, an analogy is effected between the power of a small insect and the power of a repressed people when compelled to action.

Towards an Understanding of Social Issues

Surasingh's short stories dramatize the interconnected social problems of education, health care, landless workers, tenancy, labor, indebtedness, middlemen, corruption, and even religion."Fount of Compassion" is the most explicit discussion of health care and suggests that a major cause of many village illnesses is fatigue, overwork, stress, and poor nutrition, all factors related to poverty. Poverty and poor health create a vicious cycle. Ironically, poor villagers, already under pressure to make ends meet, are forced to borrow even more money and experience even more stress in their efforts to get well. In "Daughter for Sale," the sick mother is not permitted admission to the "public" ward of the hospital, since, despite the family's large debts, they still own land. The abbot in "Fount of Compassion" supervises a thriving business that makes money off of poor people's illnesses.

In "Burmese Buddha Images," the disparity between the ideals and the practice of religion is raised in conjunction with village poverty, smuggling, and police corruption. The contrast between traditional, ideal images of Buddhism and contemporary practice are striking. In the past, the temple was the center of the community, a place of education, and an institution to which villagers donated money. Increasingly, villagers can no longer afford to create and maintain beautiful temples. In the past, Buddha images were only kept in temples or household altars; in recent years, a collector's market in art objects has arisen, in which sacred Buddha images are reduced to the status of a secular commodity. Buddhism is at its heart so opposed to the essence of capitalism that monks are not supposed to handle money directly; nor are Buddha images supposed to be bought, sold, or stolen. The climax of the story dramatizes the extent of the corruption at the heart of a Buddhist society, when heroin is transported in Buddha figures. The police, supposedly the upholders of law and order in society, destroy the Buddha images, which are both images of Buddhist values and the embodiment of the main character's capital investment.

Unsettling Conclusions

The unsettling conclusions of Surasingh's short stories challenge the conscience of the reader. The conclusion of "Amphorn's New Hope," for example, plays on the seemingly universal belief in the importance of education; however, Amphorn's new hope at the end is the beginning of the reader's feeling of hopelessness. Sure that there must be a better solution, the reader is forced to reengage the story and reconsider the telling logic of the girl's decision within her social context.

Surasingh's short stories come to an apparent close, but the issues they raise linger unresolved. His stories provide the reader with the essential data needed to comprehend his vision of the enormity of the structural problems facing Thai society. Read as a collection, his stories become a powerful statement about the direction of social change in Thailand in this period; they challenge the reader to consider the direction of future change. Rather than providing solutions, Surasingh invites the reader to critical reflection.

Thai society has undergone many changes since these short stories were written. Many idealistic students who were part of the reform movements of the 1970s are themselves now in government service, and many are trying to make improvements in Thai society. Whereas Thailand in the 1970s was only beginning the process of industrialization, government policies in the 1980s and 1990's have dramatically hastened that process. More and more villagers are being forced to leave the villages to seek alternative employment in construction work and in the manufacturing and service sectors, in low–paying and almost entirely non–unionized jobs. With the active support of the tourist industry, prostitution appears to be as widespread now as during the height of the Vietnam War, when tens of thousands of American troops were stationed in Thailand. Land speculation has driven land prices up, and more and more villagers have sold their land. How to balance urban against rural development, industrial against agricultural growth, or international trade against internal self–sufficiency are questions facing Thai society today. The fundamental problems that Surasingh poses in these short stories about Thai society in the mid–1970s are still relevant for Thailand in the 1990s.[49] Their solutions are yet to be found.

After the Short Stories

Jaturat, the magazine in which most of these collected short stories were first published, was short-lived. The magazine came to life during the brief civilian period and died along with many other publications closed down by the coup of October 6, 1976. In the days following the coup, thousands of students, workers, peasants, and other activists were arrested. It is a measure of the magazine's importance that mere possession of copies of *Jaturat* was considered sufficient cause for arrest.[50] *Jaturat*'s editor, Pansak Vinyartn, was among those arrested; other members of the magazine staff fled overseas or went into hiding.

Surasingh was among those marked for arrest in the days after the coup, both because of his role as a contributor to *Jaturat* magazine and because of his role as faculty adviser to the Chiang Mai Teachers College student council in 1975-76, a time when student activism was at its peak.[51] Police surrounded his home awaiting his return from the college. However, because he lived some twenty-five kilometers from Chiang Mai, Surasingh had a lengthy commute home and villagers were able to get word to him that it was not safe to return.

After waiting a few days for the initial tension after the coup to subside, Surasingh decided that nothing was gained by avoiding the inevitable. Charged with suspicion of "being a danger to society," he reported to the local police station. The commanding officer decided that rather than arresting him at that point, they would have him report in every week. Thus he was free to teach, but the police monitored his activities closely. Although no trial was ever held and Surasingh was never found guilty of any charges, the Teachers College suspended him and four other teachers without pay for two months. Those were very trying times for Surasingh and others in his position. They had no money with which to pay bills, and many people were afraid to communicate with them lest they too fall under suspicion.

Eventually the thousands of students, teachers, labor leaders, farmer leaders and others who had been arrested in the days following the coup were released. In most cases, no formal charges were ever filed and their cases never went to court. But for Surasingh and the others, life never returned to normal. Although Surasingh was sent to Bangkok for a one-month education program of the Internal Security Operations Command (the primary counter-insurgency agency of the Thai government at the time), a cloud of suspicion continued to hang over him.

In frustration, he requested a transfer to the Chiang Rai Teachers College, hoping the situation would improve with a new start. In 1979, he was transferred to Chiang Rai, where he taught in the Social Science and Humanities Faculty. He was then reassigned to become an assistant to the vice-rector in the research and development section. In this position, he was expected to travel from village to village throughout the northern region, interviewing villagers to assess their economic development needs. However, he became discouraged with the obstacles placed in his way and resigned from government service entirely.

Surasingh's life of new hopes and constant struggles paralleled that of the characters in his short stories. While in Chiang Rai, Surasingh began a small publishing business. In part in hopes of expanding his business opportunities and in response to pressure from his new wife who was from the adjacent city of Thonburi, Surasingh moved to Bangkok in 1983. To help make ends meet, he worked as the editorial production manager for a firm in Bangkok. As it became increasingly clear to him that he lacked sufficient financial resources, he gradually gave up his dreams of starting his own magazine.

He turned his limitless energy to working for non-government organizations (NGOs), which were beginning to flourish in Thailand in the 1980s. After a brief period with an NGO specializing in assisting handicapped children (one of his own children is deaf), he began working full-time for the German-based Friedrich Naumann Stiftung, one of the largest NGOs in Thailand at the time.

He also advised the Japanese-based Education for Development Foundation. Drawing on his tremendous knowledge of computer programming begun during his efforts in publishing, he helped various NGOs develop their computer publishing and database capabilities.

In 1991, he took a position with Southeast Asia Technology Co., Ltd., a financial consulting firm involved in development. In this new role, he participated in feasibility studies for many of the government's major development projects, ranging from the new bridge proposed in the northeastern province of Mukdahan to the deep-sea port being discussed in the southern province of Phuket.

In August of 1995, he was appointed to serve as one of six Advisors to the Minister of Industry, Chaiwat Sinsuwong.[52] A member of the Palang Dharma Party, Chaiwat was interested in promoting village-based cottage industries. With his knowledge of village life and his broad links with NGOs throughout the country, Surasingh was a promising appointment. Just when it seemed that he was finally poised to use his unusual combination of experiences to benefit villagers across the country, he learned he had liver cancer. He died in March of 1996.

Surasingh stopped writing short stories by the end of the 1970s; his last short story was "The Necklace."[53] However, his interest in literature and writing continued throughout his life, even during his years in Bangkok. From time to time, he served as a visiting professor teaching courses on Thai folklore at Thammasat and Ramkhamhaeng Universities. Until its demise, he wrote book reviews for the famous Thai magazine, Lok Nangsyy [Book World], a monthly magazine published to keep Thai intellectuals current on newly published books, both domestic and foreign. He also translated various articles, short stories, and books from English into Thai. His translations covered the spectrum from literature and history to social science. Always innovative, Surasingh even incorporated computer technology into his research on village folklore; one of his last papers (delivered at a seminar on Local Folklore Traditions at Chulalongkorn University) reported his conclusions from a computer analysis of the themes and characters in hundreds of village jokes.

He also pursued his interest in northern Thai historical texts. While teaching literature at the Chiang Mai Teachers College, he was among a vanguard of a younger generation of northern Thai intellectuals who reintroduced northern Thai palm-leaf manuscripts. Northern Thailand was historically a separate kingdom; it was only incorporated into the modern Thai state about the turn of this century. Even today northerners speak a characteristically distinct dialect of Thai. In the past, northern Thai was also a written language with a distinct script. When the government of Phibul Songkhram decreed written northern Thai to be illegal, the younger generation of northern Thai speakers were no longer able to learn to read and write the northern script. Surasingh, however, motivated by an interest in traditional northern Thai literature and history as a way to better understand the historical context of contemporary northern Thai villagers, taught himself the northern Thai script and began studying the indigenous Lannathai (as the old northern Thai kingdom was called) temple texts. As a result of his research, he published several articles on northern Thai literature and a major annotated edition of "The Path of King Kyynaa."[54]

Always eager for the latest technologies and ideas from around the world, Surasingh continued throughout his life to find new ways of combining traditional Thai practices and the latest modern innovations. He was a fascinating blend of traditional and modern, rural and urban, artist and technocrat, thinker and activist. His younger sister, reminiscing shortly before he died, commented that as a child, when other village children were playing ball, Surasingh could be found in the quiet of his room, reading. Although he had a remarkable life, Surasingh died with so much he still wanted to do. His short stories entrust the rest of us with his concerns about the everyday lives of Thai villagers.[55] Their problems still await solutions.

Notes

[1] Two other collections of translations of Thai literary works have been published by social scientists, namely, Benedict R. O'G. Anderson, a political scientist at Cornell, and Herbert Phillips, an anthropologist at Berkeley. As Phillips writes, "Literary figures are inherently interesting to an anthropologist because of their sensitive renditions of the native's viewpoint" (1987:4). He suggests that writers become in this sense "key informants."

[2] The stories not published in *Jaturat* are "Khunthong's Tomorrow," "Rit's First Mistake," "Before Dawn" and "The Necklace." "Rit's First Mistake" was published in 1979 in a collection of short stories entitled *Khlyan Hua Daeng*, edited by Suchart Sawatsri . "The Necklace" was published in 1979 in an anthology of contemporary short stories edited by Suchart Sawatsri under the title *Raakhaa Haeng Chiwit* [The Price of Life], 1979.

[3] As a graduate student in anthropology, several people had given me Surasingh's name as someone knowledgeable about village life.

[4] The *Cho Karaket* Prize was awarded annually by *Lok Nangsyy* [Book World] magazine, a Thai counterpart to the *New York Review of Books*. "The Necklace" was also the story chosen by Anderson and Mendiones for translation in their collection (1985). Unfortunately, the authors of the stories in this collection were not interviewed; and Anderson's introduction, therefore, misinterprets Surasingh's story and the meaning of its last lines (see preface).

[5] Thailand was fortunate to have been the only country in mainland Southeast Asia to avoid direct colonization. King Mongkut, well known to many Westerners as the king played by Rex Harrison in the movie "Anna and the King of Siam," is famous in Thailand for his skillful and cautious handling of these colonial powers. As King Mongkut wrote, the choice as to whether to ally with the British or the French was like deciding "whether to swim up–river to make friends with the crocodile or to swim out to sea and hang on to the whale" (Moffat 1961:124). Thailand did, however, suffer many indignities of indirect colonization, such as being forced to grant extraterritorial rights to and unequal trade arrangements with foreign powers.

[6] For an excellent discussion of the period between 1973 and 1976 and the events leading up to October 6, 1976, see Morell and Samudavanija 1981 and Mallet 1978.

[7] The Village Scouts and Red Gaurs were rightist organizations that were formed during the period after 1973.

The Village Scouts was a counter–insurgency movement that developed under the aegis of the Border Patrol Police and was subsequently given royal patronage. Several million villagers, as well as townspeople, became "village scouts." They underwent a five–day training session, involving considerable sleep deprivation, to instill nationalist sentiments. For more on this movement, see Muecke 1980; Bowie 1997.

The Red Gaurs was more of a vigilante body composed of "ex–mercenaries, school dropouts, unemployed youths and some vocational students" (Mallet 1980:84). It was formed by groups within the Internal Security Operations Command (ISOC) and other Army intelligence agencies. The Red Gaurs were associated with "the bombing and shooting of student demonstrators; harassment of labour leaders and assaulting labour strikers" (Mallett 1980:84).

[8] For more on the economic consequences of the Bowring Treaty signed between Great Britain and Siam in 1855, see Ingram 1971.

[9] For further information on the early period of American involvement, see Lobe 1977 and Randolph 1986.

[10]John Girling provides even greater detail on the financial significance of U.S. assistance to Thailand:

> The total U.S. "regular military assistance to the Thai armed forces from 1951–1971 amounted to $935.9 million. This was the equivalent to 59 percent of the total Thai military budget for the same period ($1,366.7 million). In addition, the United States provided a further $760 million in "operating costs," for acquisition of military equipment, and in payment for the Thai division in Vietnam ($200 million over four years). U.S. base construction—notably the B–52 base at Utapao, half a dozen other airfields, and the Sattahip navy facilities—amounted to a further $205 million. Finally, expenditure by U.S. military personnel in Thailand (around 50,000 at their peak in 1968–69) for rest and recreation, and other items, added a further $850 million or so (1981:236).

In addition to the 50,000 troops stationed in Thailand, there were an additional 6,500 troops each week on "rest and recreation" tours from Vietnam (Phillips 1987:6). Girling also notes the numbers of Thais directly or indirectly employed by the United States. In addition to the Thai military and police forces trained by the U.S., Girling writes, "At the peak of base construction, the United States employed, either directly or through Thai contractors, 44,000 Thais—while the livelihood of another 50,000 or more (shopowners, taxi drivers, bar girls, and hired wives) depended on the U.S. presence" (1981:236).

[11]This legislation included the Industrial Investment Promotion Act of 1962 (See Bell 1978:65).

[12]At this time the average exchange rate was twenty baht per U.S. dollar, so one baht was equivalent to about five cents.

[13]They explain the rate of inflation as follows, "Beginning in early 1973, when the US dollar was devalued by 10% while the Thai Ministry of Finance retained a 20:1 parity between the baht and the dollar, prices for commodities within Thailand began to rise rapidly. The OPEC oil increase contributed to this trend" (1981:194).

[14]Morell and Samudavanija write:

> In certain factories, especially in the textile industry, workers were still earning 12 baht a day even for an 18–hour workday (about 3.3 cents per hour). If a worker were sick, his or her wages were reduced at a rate of 20 baht per day of time off, although he or she was receiving only 12 baht a day (1981:194–195).

They also note the discrepancy between wages and profits:

> A survey by a group of Thammasat University lecturers in 1975 found the average rate of profit in the industrial sector to be 117 percent per year, the highest profit rate anywhere in Southeast Asia. In industries such as textiles, beverages, oil refining, rubber and rubber products, and pottery, the rate of profit was as high as 1000 percent (1981:195).

[15]See also Morell and Samudavanija 1981:185. Even today, over sixty percent of the country's population makes their living through agriculture.

[16]The farmers presented six points to the government, including demands for land for the 1974 planting season, permanent land for the landless, reduction of excessive interest charges, and the withdrawal of current court cases in which farmers had been charged with unwittingly using the land of absentee owners (Turton 1978:122).

[17]The formation of the FFT was a new phenomenon for rural Thailand. Before the FFT, farmers' organizations in Thailand had been under the direct control of the Ministry of Interior or the Ministry of Agriculture and Cooperatives (Turton 1978:122). See also Morell and Samudavanija 1981:222–23.

[18]While appearing to be a step forward, numerous loopholes vitiated the act's effectiveness. Enough time was provided in the act for large landowners to either sell their lands or redistribute them in such a way as to appear in compliance. Little land was actually distributed to landless villagers.

[19]A May Day gathering of peasant demonstrators was attacked by a right–wing vigilantes (the Red Gaurs) with bombs (Turton 1978: 122-123). A short time later, campaign workers for Dr. Boonsanong Punyodyana, the Secretary–General of the Socialist Party of Thailand and an active supporter of the FFT, were attacked and their vehicles set on fire when Dr. Boonsanong was running in a by–election in Chiang Mai in June 1975 (Turton 1978:122–123; for details see Bowie 1997: 153-154)).

[20]See also Bowie and Phelan 1975. For more on the FFT, see Karunan 1984.

[21]Nawaphon was a right–wing organization founded by a "group of retired and serving generals, especially in the intelligence and countersubversion branches" (Girling 1981:156). Its membership consisted of primarily "ultra–conservatives such as provincial governors, large landowners, district and village heads" (Mallet 1978:84). "Nawaphon" means "ninth force," an allusion to the King, who is also referred to as King Rama the Ninth.

[22]For an analysis of the social significance of political violence, see Anderson 1990.

[23]Morell and Samudavanija summarize events at that time:

> Grenades were thrown into crowds of people listening to political speeches, especially those of Socialist, New Force, and other leftist candidates. Precinct captains in some rural areas—again those affiliated with progressive candidates—were shot to death. A New Force party MP from Lopburi was assassinated, and the party's headquarters in Bangkok was attacked with fire bombs and partially burned. Hundreds of thousands of leaflets were distributed throughout the country accusing progressive parties and their candidates of being communists who wanted to abolish monarchy. Posters reading "All socialists are communists" appeared in many public places around Bangkok (1981:263).

[24]The army's armored division radio station (Yang Kroh), which had close links with Nawaphon, the Red Gaurs, and the Village Scouts, also played an important role in shaping public attitudes (Morell and Samudavanija 1981:274; see also Muecke 1980.)

[25]For an excellent introduction to this indigenous tradition, see Wedel and Wedel 1987. Thai scholars had, in addition, familiarized themselves with intellectual developments in other countries. Kularp Saipradit studied in Japan and Australia and returned to Thailand in 1949. He published an influential work entitled *Philosophy of Marxism* and translated many of the works of Marx and Engels (Wedel and Wedel 1987:70). Phya Anuman translated Tolstoy's *What is Art* (Reynolds 1987:35). The list of banned books in 1952 includes books by Lenin, Stalin, Engels, Gorky and Turgenev, indicating the breadth of foreign literature available in Thailand at this time (Reynolds 1987:27).

Many foreign works became accessible to Thais through Chinese avenues. China was looked to, in part, because many urban Thais are of Chinese descent and many are literate in Chinese. The Chinese communist victory in 1949 also attracted increasing interest among those seeking possible solutions to social problems in Thailand. One of the most popular Chinese writers in Thailand was Lu Xun.

[26]The origins of the phrase "Art for Life" are unclear; however in the Thai context it came to refer to a variety of arts including literature and music. The critique of "art for art's sake" is well–developed in Plekhanov's *Art and Social Life*, first published in 1912. Plekhanov, in turn, is drawing on a Marxist tradition.

Jit Phumisak became a kind of culture–hero to students during the 1970s, as much a product, according to Craig Reynolds, of the post–1973 consciousness as a cause of it (1987:16). He lived from 1930 to May 5, 1966, when he was shot by government troops. His most famous works are *Art for Life, Art for the People* and *The Real Face of Thai Feudalism*, both published under pseudonyms. For an excellent discussion on Jit Phumisak's life, see Reynolds 1987. See also Flood 1975.

Although it is not possible in the confines of this introduction to go into any detail on Jit's writing, some sense of the power of his literary skills is evidenced in the following poem:

> Each time you grab a fistful of rice
> Remember it is my sweat you swallow
> To keep on living.
> This rice has the taste
> To please the tongue of every class,
> But to grow rice is the bitter work
> That only we farmers must taste.
> From my labor the rice becomes stalks
> It takes a long, long time
> From sprout to grain
> And it is full of misery.
> Every drop of my sweat
> Reflects this hard life.
> My veins strain and bulge
> So you can eat.
> The red sweat of my labor
> Is really my life's blood
> That delights your teeth.

> Translated by Yuangrat Wedel
> (Wedel and Wedel 1987:85)

[27] Quoted from Wedel and Wedel 1987:78.

[28] In August 1974, there was an exhibition on "Literary Struggles and the 14 October Incident" at Thammasat University. In September 1974, the Social Science Association of Thailand organized a seminar on "The Thought of Jit Phumisak," with papers by such leading figures as Chonthira Kladyu, Charnvit Kasetsiri, Saneh Chamarik and Supha Sirimanonda. (For more on the intellectual climate of this period, see Reynolds 1987.)

[29] Indeed, one of Caravan's most famous songs was about Jit Phumisak.

[30] One of the most sophisticated exemplars of this new critical scholarship in English is the work of Sombat Chantornvong. See his 1981 article "Religious Literature in Thai Political Perspective: The Case of the Maha Chat Kamluang."

[31] Personal communication, Surasingh 1977.

[32] As a lecturer in a teachers college, Surasingh became interested in the broader issues of teaching and education. One of the books which influenced him most was Paolo Friere's book *Pedagogy of the Oppressed*. He was particularly interested in nonformal teaching techniques and found Friere's philosophy of education inspirational (Personal communication 1977).

[33] Personal communication 1977.

[34] *Chasbaan* (The Villager) was one of the most important progressive magazines being published at the height of the military government's power. Dealing primarily with rural issues, its core writing staff centered in the Economics Faculty at Thammasat University and included such now famous scholars such as Jermsak Phinthong, who in addition to his teaching responsibilities, hosts a regular television program broadcast nation–wide on agricultural development issues. *Chasbaan*

ties, hosts a regular television program broadcast nation–wide on agricultural development issues. *Chasbaan* was closed down by the government even before the civilian period, and *Prachathipathai* (Democracy) newspaper was shut down in 1976.

[35]Its name was well–chosen; *jaturat* literally means "square" and has wide–ranging applications ranging from "city square" to "picture frame"; the magazine focussed on, or "framed," issues of central political importance.

[36]Khamsingh Srinawk was trained in the Journalism Department of Chulalongkorn University. He is most famous for his short stories, generally published under the pseudonym Lao Khamhawm, and articles published in *Sangkhomsat Parithat* (Social Science Review). His most famous collection of short stories has been translated into English as *The Politician and Other Stories* (Srinawk 1973). He became Vice–Chairman of the Socialist Party of Thailand, which formed during the brief period of civilian government. After the coup of 1976, he briefly joined the Communist Party of Thailand until differences led him to break with the CPT in 1977.

Sulak Sivaraksa was trained as a lawyer in England. For a time he worked for the BBC and taught at the School of Oriental and African Studies (SOAS) in London. Upon his return to Thailand, he became involved in a variety of activities. He is President of Suksit Siam Bookstore and Board Member of the Siam Society. He started the famous *Sangkhomsat Parithat* (Social Science Review). His books published in English include *Siamese Resurgence* (1985) and *A Socially Engaged Buddhism* (1988).

[37]The famous Thai human rights lawyer Thongbai Thongpao and others have formed a group to put pressure on the government to track down the murderers of those journalists who have been assassinated.

[38]See Rutnin 1988:21; Senanan 1975:63–64; Seriwat 1977 (quoted in Anderson 1985:12).

[39]Rutnin describes the circumstances of the uproar engendered by the publication of "Sanuk Nyk":

> It is a story about four monks of Wat Boworniwet discussing their future plans before leaving the monkhood. The abbot took it as a direct insult to his wat. He immediately submitted his resignation to the king. The king had to write a personal letter of apology to him and explain that the author was only imitating the farang ("Western") fiction purely for entertainment, and had no intention of writing a true story. The prince was later reprimanded by the king. (1988:21).

[40]Personal communication 1978; Interview with Surasingh, November 2, 1989.

[41]A similar issue is raised in the discussion of the writing of history. As Macaulay, the famous English historian wrote:

> Perfectly and absolutely true [history] cannot be; for, to be perfectly and absolutely true, it ought to record all the slightest particulars of the slightest transaction—all the things done and all the words uttered during the time of which it treats. The omission of any circumstance, however insignificant, would be a defect. If history were written thus, the Bodleian library would not contain the occurrences of a week...
>
> History has its foreground and its background; and it is principally in the management of its perspective that one artist differs from another (Stern 1972:76–77).

[42]Mencher notes four primary techniques: 1) scene by scene reconstruction, involving moving from place to place to witness events as they occurred; 2) full, extensive, and realistic dialogue; 3) use of third–person point–of–view based on interviews in which people's feelings are described, and 4) meticulous social observation (1977:440).

Many of the ideas and techniques of New Journalism have been incorporated into modern journalism today, with the increased use of profiles, interviews, and descriptions of the setting for heightened drama that are now commonplace in newspaper articles or on the evening news. It has given reporters greater freedom in both subject matter and writing style.

[43]Herbert Phillips notes, "The concepts of 'journalists as culture hero' and 'journalist–cum–creative writer' are by no means unique to Thailand. The latter runs both deep and strong in the Western world where there are such varied examples as Daniel Defoe, Charles Dickens, Mark Twain, Sinclair Lewis, George Orwell, Ernest Hemingway, and Albert Camus" (1987:75). To this list can be added Walt Whitman, John Greenleaf Whittier, Edgar Allan Poe, Stephan Crane, Theodore Dreiser, Carl Sandburg, and many others.

Well–known Thai writers who also work as journalists include Kularp Saipradit, Jit Phumisak, Thongbai Thongpao, Suchit Wongthet, Sulak Sivaraksa, Suchart Sawatsri, Khamsingh Srinawk, Witthayakorn Chiangkun, and even Thailand's most famous literary figure M.R. Kukrit Pramoj, the founder of Siam Rath newspaper and former Prime Minister of Thailand. For more on Kukrit Pramoj, see Manivat, Van Beek 1983. For details on other writers, see Anderson 1985, Wedel and Wedel 1987, and Phillips 1987.

[44]Personal communication 1977.

[45]Interview with Surasingh, November 2, 1989.

[46]Interview with Surasingh, November 2, 1989. Confronting the similar issue of writing about atrocities as non–fiction, Michael Taussig (1987) gives a fascinating and moving account of the difficulties of writing about the torture and killing of Indian rubber–gatherers in Columbia by the Peruvian Amazon Company.

[47]The fisherman in this story, in fact, refers back to the lead character in "A Curse on Your Paddyfields."

[48]Interview with Surasingh, November 2, 1989.

[49]An excellent discussion of contemporary social issues facing Thailand in the 1990s can be found in Ekachai 1990 and 1994.

[50]Despite its wide circulation and importance, none of the libraries in Thailand has a complete set of this magazine, Copies survive in private collections. Cornell University in Ithaca, New York is one of the few libraries that has copies of *Jaturat*.

[51]Surasingh was a very active and well-liked teacher. Earlier, when he had been teaching at Nakhon Sri Thammarat, he had been awarded a double promotion for outstanding work in 1975. His rapport with students took many forms. Among them was being asked to become the faculty advisor to the students during the 1975-76 period, when student activism was increasing and students were involved in a range of social issues, not the least of which was the farmers' movement.

[52] Surasingh was a friend of Chaiwat Surawichai since childhood days in Lampang. A student leader, Chaiwat Surawichai was one of the group of thirteen arrested in 1973 for demanding a constitution. A fellow northerner, Chaiwat became deputy-head of the Socialist Party of Thailand. In recent years, he has been serving as a member of the secretarial committee of the Palang Dharma Party. Because of his friendship with Chaiwat Surawichai, Surasingh agreed to become an advisor to Chaiwat Sinsuwong, even though Surasingh never became a formal member of the Palang Dharma Party.

[53]After the coup of October 6, Surasingh virtually stopped writing short stories. Two of the stories included in this collection, "Khunthong's Tomorrow" and "Before Dawn," were never published; they had been written for *Jaturat*, but the magazine was closed down before they could be printed. "Instinctive Mistake" was written shortly after the coup, but not published until later in an anthology of short stories.

[54]*Khong Jyy Haeng Prachaw Kyynaa* (Bangkok: Sukanya Press, 1985). Interest in indigenous texts has been growing dramatically in recent years, and the vanguard of intellectuals, of which Suras-

ingh was an important member, has been producing fascinating work. Foreign foundations, primarily German and Japanese, have contributed funds in the past few years, making it possible to preserve these indigenous palm-leaf manuscripts on microfilms for future generations of scholars.

[55]As the recent articles written by Sanitsuda Ekachai, a renowned Thai journalist, reveal, the problems caused by political and economic inequality continue. See Sanitsuda Ekachai's *Behind the Smile: Voices of Thailand* (Bangkok: Thai Development Support Committee, 1990) and *Seeds of Hope: Local Initiatives in Thailand* (Bangkok: Thai Development Support Committee, 1994).

References

Anderson, Benedict. 1977. Withdrawal Symptoms: Social and Cultural Aspects of the October 6 Coup. *Bulletin of Concerned Asian Scholars* 9, no.3:13–30.

_____, 1990. Murder and Progress in Modern Siam. *New Left Review*, May/June:33–48.

_____, and Ruchira Mendiones, eds. and trans. 1985. *In the Mirror: Literature and Politics in Siam in the American Era*. Bangkok: Duang Kamol.

Bell, Peter F. 1978. "Cycles" of Class Struggle in Thailand. In *Thailand: Roots of Conflict*, ed. Andrew Turton, Jonathan Fast and Malcolm Caldwell. Nottingham: Spokesman.

Botan. 1982. *Letters from Thailand*. Susan Fulop, trans. Bangkok: Duang Kamol.

Bowie, Katherine. 1997. *Rituals of National Loyalty: An Anthropology of the State and the Village Scout Movement in Thailand*. New York: Columbia University Press.

Bowie, Katherine and Brian Phelan. 1975. Who is Killing the Farmers? *Bangkok Post Sunday Magazine*, August 17.

Cadet, John M. 1975. *The Ramakien: The Stone Rubbings of the Thai Epic*. New York: Kodansha International.

Chaloemtiarana, Thak. 1979. *Thailand: The Politics of Despotic Paternalism*. Bangkok: Thammasat University, Thai Khadi Institute.

Chantornvong, Sombat. 1981. Religious Literature in Thai Political Perspective: The Case of the Maha Chat Kamluang. In *Essays on Literature and Society in Southeast Asia*, ed. Tham Seong Chee, 187–205. Singapore: Singapore University Press.

Chee, Tham Seong, ed. 1981. *Essays on Literature and Society in Southeast Asia*. Singapore: Singapore University Press.

Chitkasem, Manas. 1972. The Emergence and Development of the Nirat Genre in Thai Poetry. Journal of the Siam Society 60, part 2 (July): 135–168.

Draskau, Jennifer. 1975. *Taw and Other Short Stories*. Hong Kong: Heinemann Educational Books.

Ekachai, Sanitsuda. 1990. *Behind the Smile: Voices of Thailand*. Bangkok: Thai Development Support Committee.

_____. 1994. *Seeds of Hope: Local Initiatives in Thailand*. Bangkok: Post Publishing Co Ltd.

Flood, Thadeus. 1975. The Thai Left Wing in Historical Context. *Bulletin of Concerned Asian Scholars* 7, no.2: 55–67.

Freire, Paolo. 1986. *Pedagogy of the Oppressed*. Transl. by Myra Bergman Ramos. New York: Continuiuim.

Girling, John L. S. 1981. *Thailand: Society and Politics*. Ithaca: Cornell University Press.

Heinze, Ruth–Inge. 1974. Ten Days in October—Students vs. the Military. *Asian Survey* 14, no. 6: 491–508.

Ingersoll, Fern S., ed. 1973. *Sang Thong: A Dance Drama From Thailand, written by King Rama II and the Poets of His Court*. Rutland: Charles E. Tuttle Co.

Ingram, James C. 1971. *Economic Change in Thailand*, 1850–1970. Palo Alto: Stanford University Press.

Jumsai, M. L. Manich. 1973. *History of Thai Literature*. Bangkok: Chalermnit.

Karunan, Victor P. 1984. *A History of Peasant Movements in Thailand and the Philippines*. Hong Kong: Plough Publications.

Kasetsiri, Charnvit. 1979. Thai Historiography from Ancient Times to the Modern Period. *In Perceptions of the Past in Southeast Asia*, ed. A. J. S. Reid and D. G. Marr, 156–170. Hong Kong: Heinemann.

Keyes, Charles F. 1989. *Thailand: Buddhist Kingdom as Modern Nation–State*. Boulder: Westview Press.

Kladyu, Chontira. 1974. *People's Literature* (Wannakhadi khong Puangchon). Bangkok: Academic Section, Chulalongkorn University Student Club.

Kobjitti, Chart. 1983. *The Judgement.* TraLaurie Maund, transl. Bangkok: Thammasat University.

Mailer, Norman. 1968. *Armies of the Night: History as a Novel, the Novel as History.* New York: New American Library.

Malakul, M.L. Pin. 1975. Dramatic Achievement of King Rama VI. *Journal of the Siam Society* 63, part 2 (July): 264–71.

Mallet, Marian. 1978. Causes and Consequences of the October '76 Coup. *In Thailand: Roots of Conflict,* ed. Andrew Turton, Jonathan Fast, and Malcolm Caldwell. Nottingham: Spokesman.

Manivat, Vilas, comp. and Steve Van Beek, ed. 1983. *Kukrit Pramoj, His Wit and Wisdom: Writings, Speeches and Interviews.* Bangkok: Duang Kamol.

Marx, Karl and Friedrich Engels. 1976. *On Literature and Art.* Moscow: Progress Publishers.

Masavisut, Nitaya, ed. 1984. *Thai P.E.N Anthology: Short Stories and Poems of Social Consciousness.* Bangkok: P.E.N. International Thailand Center.

McCoy, Alfred W. 1972. *The Politics of Heroin in Southeast Asia.* New York: Harper and Row.

Mencher, Melvin. 1977. *News Reporting and Writing.* Dubuque, Iowa: William C. Brown, Publ.

Moffat, Abbot Low. 1961. *Mongkut, the King of Siam. Ithaca*: Cornell University Press.

Morell, David and Chai–anan Samudavanija. 1981. *Political Conflict in Thailand: Reform, Reaction, Revolution.* Cambridge: Oelgeschlager, Gunn and Hain, Publ., Inc.

Muecke, Marjorie A. 1980. The Village Scouts of Thailand. *Asian Survey* 20 (4): 407–427.

Phillips, Herbert P. 1987. *Modern Thai Literature, with an Ethnographic Interpretation*. Honolulu: University of Hawaii Press.

Phu, Sunthorn. 1986. *Nirat Phra Prathom*. Montri Umavijani, tr. Bangkok: Amarin Press.

Plekhanov, G. V. 1957. *Art and Social Life*. Moscow: Progress Publishers.

Poolthupya, Srisurang. 1981. Social Change as Seen in Modern Thai Literature. In *Essays on Literature and Society in Southeast Asia*. Ed. Tham Seong Chee, 206–215. Singapore: Singapore University Press.

Pramoj, Kukrit. 1981. *Si Phaendin: Four Reigns*. Two volumes. Tulachandra, tr. Bangkok: Duang Kamol.

Randolph, R. Sean. 1979. The Limits to Influence: American Aid to Thailand, 1965–1970. *Asian Affairs* 6 (4): 243–266.

Reynolds, Craig J. 1987. *Thai Radical Discourse and The Real Face of Thai Feudalism Today*. Ithaca: Cornell University Southeast Asia Program.

Rutnin, Mattani Mojdara. 1988. *Modern Thai Literature*. Bangkok: Thammasat University Press.

Sawatsri, Suchart. 1979. *Raakhaa Haeng Chiwit*. Bangkok: Duang Kamol.

———, ed. 1979. *Khlyan Hua Daeng*. Bangkok: Duang Kamol.

———, ed. 1979. *Raakhaa Haeng Chiwit*.

Senanan, Wibha. 1975. *The Genesis of the Novel in Thailand*. Bangkok: Thai Wattana Panich.

Shimbhanao, Surasinghsamruam. 1977. *Kaanlalen Khong Dek Lannathai* [Traditional Northern Thai Children's Games]. Chiang Mai: Suun Nangsyy Chiang Mai.

Simmonds, E.H.S. 1963. Thai Narrative Poetry: Palace and Provincial Texts of an Episode from Khun Chang Khun Phaen. *Asia Major* 10, pt. 2: 279–299.

Sivaraksa, Sulak. 1985. *Siamese Resurgence*. Bangkok: Suksit Siam.

_____. 1988. *A Socially Engaged Buddhism*. Bangkok: Thai Inter–Religious Commission for Development.

Srinawk, Khamsing [Lao Khamhawm]. 1973. *The Politician and Other Short Stories*. Transl. Domnern Garden, ed. Michael Smithies. Oxford in Asia Modern Authors Series. New York: Oxford University Press.

Stern, Fritz, ed. 1972. *The Varieties of History: From Voltaire to the Present*. New York: Vintage Books.

_____. 1985. *Khong Jyy Haeng Prachaw Kyynaa* [The Path of King Kyynaa]. Bangkok: Sukanya Press.

Taussig, Michael. 1987. *Shamanism, Colonialism, and the Wild Man: A Study in Terror and Healing*. Chicago: University of Chicago Press.

Turton, Andrew. 1978. The Current Situation in the Thai Countryside. In *Thailand: Roots of Conflict*, ed. Andrew Turton, Jonathan Fast, and Malcolm Caldwell. Nottingham: Spokesman.

_____, Jonathan Fast, and Malcolm Caldwell, eds. 1978. *Thailand: Roots of Conflict*. Nottingham: Spokesman.

Van der Meer, C. L. J. 1981. *Rural Development in Northern Thailand: An Interpretation and Analysis*. Groningen: Krips Repro Meppel.

Wedel, Yuangrat, with Paul Wedel. 1987 *Radical Thought, Thai Mind: The Development of Revolutionary Ideas in Thailand*. Bangkok: Assumption Business Administration College.

Wijewardene, Gehan, transl. 1982. *The Teachers of Mad Dog Swamp*. New York: University of Queensland Press.

Wolf, Thomas. 1968. *The Electric Kool–Aid Acid Test*. New York: Farrar, Straus, & Giroux.

The Stories

A Curse on Your Paddyfields

The soft billowing green of planted paddyfields gives most people who look at them a feeling of harmony and renewal. But there is another group of people who can hardly wait for the rice and other crops of silver and gold to disappear from the land as quickly as possible. They have no interest in whether crop yields are high or low, or whether there are any yields at all.

Because once the crops have been harvested and removed from the fields, the lands that appear useless once again become public property. Anyone can go and gather animals and plants of all kinds without owners getting upset. Lizards, mice, toads, frogs, fish, and even dung–beetles have been the delicacies of the poor for generations. In addition, there are edible plants of all descriptions, such as *haew, phak bung, phak waen, phak khiikhuang and phak ihin.*[*] These plants and animals have never had landlords or tenants disputing ownership over them.

This rainy season, just before the farmers began plowing up the land and before the young people came home from their jobs in the city, Kham had been able to catch more fish in the paddyfields than ever before. He had sold so many fish that he had accumulated quite a sum of money. After consulting with *Paa* Phuang, his life partner, *Lung* Kham was finally able to buy something he had wanted for as long as he could remember. He had wanted it so badly that he had already given up attaining it in this lifetime.

Every other rainy season *Lung* Kham had despaired, thinking if he only had a Mida[†] lantern, he would be certain to find more fish than anyone else. The best way to find fish in the paddyfields was with a light to illuminate the water and a finely woven cage in which to trap the fish as they lay sleeping in the night. But with the dim light from his tin-can kerosene lamp and vision blurred with age, he could not rival the youngsters who used bright Mida lanterns.

---

[*]These plants, eaten fresh or cooked with pickled fish, fermented soybeans, or chilies, are an important part of many villagers diet. The tubular roots of the *haew* plant are sweet and rich in starch. *Phak bung* is a kind of morning glory. *Phak waen* and *phak khiikhuang* are creeping ground plants, the former found in swamps, ponds, and paddyfields, the latter in drier places. *Phak ihin* is an aquatic herb.

[†]Mida is the trade name of a Japanese kerosene lantern similar to a Coleman lamp.

Many of his neighbors watched jealously as *Lung* Kham stroked, touched, caressed, and polished his brand–new Mida lantern that he had just bought from Chinaman Mong for nearly 300 baht. Actually his lantern was a different brand than Mida, but everyone still called it by that name anyway, including Chinaman Mong.

He was so engrossed, so enraptured with his new Mida that *Paa* Phuang had to remind him to go and check the fish traps that he had set earlier.

It was long after they had finished supper that evening when *Paa* Phuang finally decided to permit Daeng, their eldest son who was just entering fourth grade that year, to go fishing with his father.

Daeng had begged to go fishing at night with his father many times before, but both *Lung* Kham and *Paa* Phuang had told him the same thing each time. The glow of a single kerosene lamp wasn't sufficient to light the way for both Daeng and his father at the same time.

After getting dressed, with some delays lighting the lantern, father and son left home, setting off for the paddyfields. The fields had already been partly plowed, so there were no more weeds left; it would be easier now to see the fish.

The lights of different kinds of lanterns of the other fish hunters twinkled all over the horizon and were redoubled by their reflection in the mirror–still water.

Lung Kham carried the lantern in his left hand and a fish cage in his right. A large basket to hold the captured fish hung over his hip. Ever so carefully he took one step after the other, wading cautiously in the calf–deep water. Daeng carried his bamboo fish cage in his left hand. In his right hand he carried a big knife about a half–meter in length. He walked on the left–hand side of his father and just as cautiously.

The gazes of both were transfixed, peering into the water. Their ears hardly heard the sound of frogs and toads croaking noisily about them in all directions. Dozens of fish–eater snakes stuck their heads out of the water, motionless. They stared imperviously at their two human competitors, who in turn viewed them with equally little emotion.

"Daeng, you can't use the cage for eels or scorpion fish, or they will escape. You have to stun them with the knife. Come down straight on top of their heads with all your might. Cut through the water with the sharp edge of the knife, not the broad side. Here, I'll show you how."

The young red–colored eel the width of a thumb lay stretched out full–length in the water, so still it seemed to be already dead. The sharp edge of the knife came down on its neck, driving its head into the soft mud. It jerked around in every direction, muddying the water. Before the surrounding water could clear, the eel had been picked up and put into the basket of the little boy.

already, there's a chance you'll hit it so hard it may die. Then we can't get a good price for it. You have to hit them just right. You can't let any marks show either. And don't do anything careless like hitting a snake. Look carefully before you strike. If you hit a snake, it means that all night long we'll have no hope of catching any more fish. Harming snakes brings bad luck."

"Daeng, Daeng! Come here quickly and hold the Mida for me. Here's a full–grown *duk** fish. They're very hard to catch. Other fish you just have to trap under the cage and then reach in and grab them. But *duk* fish of this size take patience. Sometimes you have to wait a long time for the right moment to grab them. Otherwise they can give you a wound that throbs for days."

*   *   *

The planting of the paddyfields marks the end of the golden age for villagers such as *Lung* Kham. Then the fertile womb of the paddyfield, which had been virtually public domain, reverts to private property. The owners guard their individual plots jealously, lest the tender rice seedlings be harmed. No longer can anyone roam through the waters looking for fish. *Lung* Kham and others of his class knew this unwritten law of their fellow villagers only too well and never thought to violate it .

Only a single patch of swamp located at the far edge of the paddyfields remained out of all of *Lung* Kham's fishing places; it, too, would dry up in the dry season. Then he would have to walk along the bunds in the paddyfields, taking his beloved lantern. He would also take along another implement, a bamboo stick the width of his index finger and about one meter long. Its forked tip was interwoven with bamboo into a board used for hitting frogs.

Lung Kham didn't like earning a living by catching frogs. The frogs' expression when hit on the head was awful. It tormented him to see their tears flow and their two front legs reach up to their eyes to wipe them away. But *Lung* Kham and others in his position had ever fewer choices.

The night arrived that *Lung* Kham knew was the last night he could hunt fish in the paddyfields before he would have to change his form of livelihood to foraging in the forest. That night his basket had fewer fish, crabs, frogs, and

---

*A *duk* is small variety of catfish with sharp poisonous fins. Timing is important in catching these fish, the palm of the hand coming over its head and the second and third fingers coming around, but avoiding, its fins. If cut by its fins, villagers traditionally believe one must see a spirit doctor to extract the poison lest one die.

clams than ever, so few that he feared they would not make up for the cost of the kerosene he was using for his lantern.

As he paused to set the lantern on the path through the paddyfield to pump more air into it, he caught sight of a *chohn*** fish. It was as wide as his wrist. Hiding among the ricestalks now over half a meter high, it lay so still that one almost might not think it was a fish. *Lung* Kham hesitated for a moment. If he used his fishtrap, he was afraid that, in the process, he might damage some of the rice shoots. Instead, he decided to get a firm grasp on his knife and came down with all his might on its head. He made such a loud noise that he startled even himself. The water became murky with mud and blood, but the *chohn* fish was no longer there. Instead, the sound of the writhing fish came from the middle of the ricefield. *Lung* Kham set off after the fish. He carefully waded between the rows of planted ricestalks, looking right and left, careful not to injure any of the seedlings, not wanting any of the plants to be damaged by him.

Suddenly a gunshot rang out across the paddyfields. The lantern in his hand shattered. He was terrified. A cold shiver ran down his spine. His heart fluttered. When he came to his senses, he took off, running for dear life, his two legs so light that he didn't notice them. The rice shoots in his path were trampled underfoot. From the distance, he heard a voice yelling out after him.

"You cur! Trampling everything down! So it's you who have been ruining the rice! Now I'll have to replant it all over again, and I don't have enough money to buy more seedlings. If I find you here again, I'll shoot you dead!"

---

*A *chohn* has a head like a snake and is one of the strongest freshwater fish, able to jump long distances and swim well. A big *chohn* has been known to jump straight at the chest of a man bending to catch it, such that he was knocked out by the force of the blow and drowned in the water.

Daughter for Sale

After he gave his word to *Yai* Phloy, *Lung* Maa couldn't think of what to tell his daughter. His heart ached, knowing that the words *Yai* Phloy had uttered that day were outright lies. But what was he to have done? No matter what, he would have to let his daughter go with *Yai* Phloy. So what point would there have been in disagreeing with her, in forcing her to speak the truth? Wouldn't he only be degrading himself by admitting openly for everyone to hear that he was so destitute that he had to sell his daughter. Far better to let *Yai* Phloy go on with her eloquent deception. However wrong, he could then mumble that he had been tricked by *Yai* Phloy. In any event, a man is better branded as having been conned than branded as having sold his daughter into prostitution.

Yai Phloy's soliloquy was most persuasive. Anyone listening to it would have been seduced by it. *Yai* Phloy began by elucidating in great detail about how children's behavior these days was getting steadily worse and worse, especially city children, and especially in Bangkok. This was because their parents were so busy working, striving to get ahead, that they had no time to stay at home with their children. Instead, the children were ignored until they finally got into trouble. Hiring someone to take care of the children was extremely difficult. Some hired servants who, as soon as their employers weren't watching, absconded with everything in the house. Lots of them stole, even if just a little here and there. But the major problem was that servants were so unreliable. As soon as they were the least bit tired or were criticized or scolded in the least, they ran away back to their homes. Consequently, several of Bangkok's wealthy elite had requested *Yai* Phloy to find them dependable girls to be their servants. They paid good wages and, moreover, even paid money in advance. As many girls as she could get would be placed.

Even though *Yai* Phloy was not from his village, *Lung* Maa had known *Yai* Phloy since she had been a young girl. In those days, her beauty was known throughout the subdistrict. But before any of the local youths were able to compete for possession, *Yai* Phloy had already run off to Bangkok with someone who had passed through with the medicine show.* Much, much later, when she finally came back, word had it that she had become thoroughly Bangkokian, with a haughty manner and pretentious lifestyle. She appeared to have become a lady of no insignificant wealth. *Yai* Phloy went back and forth to Bangkok often. Of the girls that went to Bangkok with her, some came back wealthy, others came back even poorer than before. And some disappeared completely.

Lung Maa knew perfectly well what kind of work the girls who went with *Yai* Phloy did in Bangkok, because one day he had gone to get an injection at the district health center. That day, the only too discreet doctor there had told him that two or three of the girls who had gone to Bangkok with *Yai* Phloy had come back with severe cases of gonorrhea, so severe that he had had to send them into town for treatment.

Lung Maa heaved a deep sigh as he thought of his daughter who was soon to become one more in the ranks of unlucky girls. He wanted to talk with his daughter so she would understand and be as untroubled as possible. But he could think of nothing to say.

Paa Saeng, his partner through life, was lying sick in the hospital in the city, suffering from an intestinal problem. She was waiting for the money that would be used to pay for the blood and surgery needed to sustain her life. Her survival, though, would only continue her pain and suffering.

He couldn't borrow money from anyone else any more. His present debt totalled already about 10,000 baht. He'd been in debt for nearly ten years. In all those years, all his efforts had only succeeded in ensuring that his debts compounded interest slowly.

One year, the garlic price had been exceptionally good, which was why he found himself in his present state. The merchants that year had come directly to the village, buying at fourteen to fifteen baht a kilo. It meant that, for once, *Lung* Maa had had enough money to think of working for a better life. So, he borrowed 10,000 baht. With that and the money he had saved previously, he bought another three rai of paddyfield. He was willing to pay the interest rate of 150 *thang*† of rice per year. He had planned to use the entire rice crop from the newly bought land to pay the interest and use the money from the dry season crop to pay off the original loan.

---

*Traditionally, medicines were sold at the showing of free movies. The youths who sold the medicines were rumored to be pimps as well, who deceived young village girls with words of love and promises of a new life and then sold them into prostitution.

†The interest rate mentioned in this story is, in fact, lower than that being charged in many villages in the north during the 1970s, where rates of 25-30 *thang* per 1,000 baht borrowed per year was the normal rate. In 1977 the rice price per *thang* was, at the harvest time (the cheapest price of any time in the year), 20-25 baht per *thang*, or a cash equivalent interest of 775 baht or 77.5% (an interest rate almost equal to the amount borrowed), and was payable every year until the original debt was repaid. One *rai* yields 30-60 *thang* per crop.

But he met with bad luck. The following year, the garlic prices dropped to between thirty and fifty *satang* a kilo, despite his effort to appease the merchants by bringing the garlic directly to their warehouses and despite the fact that the seed he had bought had been very expensive, nearly fifty baht a kilo. He thought they were probably garlic seeds imported from China. That year began his downward cycle. No matter how he struggled by trying other crops, the profit he made was only enough to see his family through. One year, the price of rice dropped to five baht a *thang,* forcing him to give up his new plot of land to his creditor. But he was still left with debts worth more than the plot of land he had inherited from his parents. His debts kept steadily increasing. Now he was working his remaining four *rai* without getting anything himself, because the rice yield went to pay the interest on his debts. The hope that he would one day clear himself of his debts had faded.

As he thought of his past, his eyes brimmed with tears of bitterness at his fate, welling over as his thoughts turned to the future. In another two or three days, his daughter, while still living, would be forced into hell in Bangkok. In two or three more weeks, he would once again face the painful sight of his creditor callously coming to collect 200 *thang* of rice. This year there had not been enough water, so he was not sure if he would have enough rice to pay, and if there would be any left over. Agony tore his heart as he recalled the words of his creditor, echoing in his mind: "Maa, the money you've borrowed from me now amounts to more than the value of the land you mortgaged. What am I to do? If it keeps on like this, I'm afraid I'm going to have to ask to claim your land and house. Next year my son is going abroad, so I'll be having a lot of expenses myself. So please try to pay me by then, if even only the interest."

*　　*　　*

So now his daughter had gone with *Yai* Phloy. He had controlled his tears. His parting words to his daughter had been to obey *Yai* Phloy without questions. If she had any problems, she should write a letter and let him know. He consoled her by saying if he had a chance, he would come to visit her. Of what he had prepared to tell her, not a single word came out.

The 2,500 baht he had received as an advance from *Yai* Phloy was barely enough to pay for *Paa* Saeng's hospital expenses. And when *Paa* Saeng returned home and learned that her daughter had gone off with *Yai* Phloy, she fainted instantly. When she recovered, she began sobbing and sobbing. She wouldn't talk to or even look *Lung* Maa in the face, let alone any of her other five children who were standing around her. *Lung* Maa could think of nothing to say, so he sought silent refuge in making bamboo ties.[*]

---

[*]The harvested rice is bound together in preparation for threshing with long ties made of bamboo.

Late that night, when all their children were asleep, *Paa* Saeng's voice, muffled with the sounds of weeping, whispered, "*Phii* Maa, didn't you know what *Ee* Phloy took our daughter off to do?"

"Mother, I knew, but it was necessary. You know as well as I that we had no choice. When you were in the hospital, if we didn't have the money to pay for the cost of the medicine, the blood, the saline, and other expenses, the doctor wouldn't have been willing to treat you. They wouldn't let us go to the destitute ward.* Are you angry with me?"

"No, I'm not angry. But I feel so sad. Ever since I was born, there's been nothing but suffering."

"Do you know *Yai* Phloy well?"

"Oh, the people in the market place know her only too well. She's taken several of their daughters to sell already. She gets paid 500 baht a head for some, 2-300 baht for others. She takes whatever she can get. She's been a prostitute herself, ever since she was young. When she was no longer able to sell herself, she began selling young girls instead. Her parents had a lot of debts then. Now things seem to be going better for them, but they still owe money."

"I worry about our daughter. I feel so sorry for her. Ever since she left, I don't sleep at night."

"*Phii* Maa, the matter has happened and nothing can be done, so we might as well let it pass. We'll help each other to share the burden of our demerit. It's just as if she has gone off and gotten a husband, only that she doesn't have a real husband ... By the time she can earn the money to help her parents, I wonder how many husbands she will have had..."

---

* A person with assets such as land is not considered destitute and therefore not eligible.

Escaping the Middleman

The limes in her garden were so ripe that their bright yellow shone through the trees. If left on the trees another two or three days they'd start dropping off and wouldn't be worth as much. *Paa* Saaj decided she couldn't wait any longer for someone to come to the village to buy limes. She and her children picked the limes that were ripe, many of them almost over-ripe, filling two baskets to the brim. She planned to sell them early the next morning at the weekend market.

Paa Saaj didn't like going to the weekend market at all. The trip there and back would cost her ten baht. She'd have to get up before daybreak and leave the housework and chores for the children to do. Actually, there were several other markets closer to her village, but who there would buy two full baskets of limes? The people who went to those markets were peasant villagers like herself.

She took the opportunity to gather *tamlyng*[*] plants she'd been growing in her garden and tied them into bunches. Then *Paa* Saaj left her home and walked over to the home of *Paa* Dii, who lived four houses away from her. *Paa* Dii could have the mini–truck pick the two of them up at the same time. But, *Paa* Dii wasn't home, and she left word with *Paa* Dii's son.

Her husband returned home from the paddyfields and saw the baskets prepared for the market. He was worried that they were far too heavy for her to carry. But *Paa* Saaj insisted that if she only took a small number, it wouldn't cover the cost of the trip.

The next morning, as the cocks began their crowing, *Paa* Saaj hurriedly got up, steamed rice for the family, and wrapped some in a banana–leaf to take to eat at the market. No sooner had she finished, than the mini–truck arrived and beeped its horn at the gate.

"Coming!" she shouted back as she lifted her baskets and hurried to the truck. She staggered several times under the weight.

---

[*] *Tamlyng (cucurbitaceae)* is a herbaceous climber, common on hedge rows and thickets. The young tender part of the climber is edible.

The noise of the truck engine, the babble of chattering women, and the incessant jostling made it difficult to carry on a conversation with *Paa* Dii. The back of the truck was crammed full, women and baskets squashed together. Entrusting herself to *Paa* Dii's care, *Paa* Saaj didn't feel like talking. Not long after the truck reached the black–topped road, the women in the truck began dropping off to sleep.

"Saaj, Saaj. We're almost there. Get your things ready. Did you bring a flashlight or lamp with you?"

"No, I didn't ..."

"Well, that's a bit of a problem. You'll just have to follow me," *Paa* Dii said as she got ready to get out.

The truck came to a stop and the market women pushed and shoved each other as each tried to get out first. The driver hurried to help unload the women's baskets. Flashlights blinked in all directions.

"We've arrived late this morning. Now the other sellers will have taken up all the spaces," a woman shouted, scolding the driver.

"What do you mean late? It's not even 5 a.m. yet!" a voice shouted back.

Paa Dii grabbed her carrying pole and empty baskets and darted off into the crowd. Though *Paa* Saaj couldn't see her, she heard *Paa* Dii's voice calling back to her, "Saaj, follow me, but hurry up!"

By the time the driver finally lifted her baskets down from the top of the car, *Paa* Saaj could only vaguely make out the back of *Paa* Dii. *Paa* Saaj shifted her two baskets into position and was putting the carrying pole in between to lift them onto her shoulder when suddenly the beam of a flashlight lit up both her baskets.

"*Paa*, what are you selling those vegetables for?" A hand reached down and picked up a bunch.

"One *salyng* each."

"What about two bunches for one *salyng*? Then I'd buy the whole lot."

Paa Saaj hesitated. Her eyes searched for *Paa* Dii, but couldn't find her in the darkness.

"What about it, *Paa*? Each bunch is so small. They aren't even the green–tipped kind. These white–tipped ones can't be kept very long."

Bewildered, *Paa* Saaj considered what she should do. It was true; she hadn't bought them. But she had taken a lot of time and work to gather enough plants to make just one bunch.

"No, these vegetables were just freshly picked at dusk yesterday."

"So what will you come down to, *Paa*? I'm buying them to sell. You should divide some of your profit with me."

"Three for fifty *satang*. That's the cheapest possible price."

"I'll give you one baht for seven. Remember, I'm taking the whole lot. Hmm, you have fifteen bundles here. Here's two baht. Here, take the money, *Paa*."

Two baht were forced into *Paa* Saaj's palm. The *tamlyng* plants were transferred into the buyer's baskets, who then got ready to walk off. Stunned, *Paa* Saaj held the money and watched the figure of the buyer walking away. She felt dissatisfied.

Another flashlight shone on her baskets. The flashlight's owner squatted down next to her, hands rummaging among the limes while she looked up and asked *Paa* Saaj, "*Maekhaa*, how much per hundred limes?"

"Ten baht." *Paa* Saaj squatted down, looking the other woman in the face.

"Oh ho? So expensive? No one will buy them at that price! Try another price."

"Ten baht is not expensive. There aren't many limes this season, so they're hard to come by."

"Really far too expensive! And they're such small limes, too. They're already going bad. They can't be kept much longer before they'll rot. Look at those. I bought those for seven baht per hundred, no more. Here, have a look. And they're much better looking, too."

Paa Saaj peered at the limes inside the woman's bag. She hadn't had a chance to get a proper look when the light flashed back to her limes.

"So what do you say? Give me another offer. If it's not too high, I'll buy the whole lot."

"How much are you willing to give me?" *Paa* Saaj asked in frustration.

"Six baht," she said, while preparing to stand up. "All right, I'll give you eight."

"That's one more baht than the price they've been buying them for in the village," *Paa* Saaj thought to herself.

"Actually that's too much. I'll have a look around and come back later. At that price no one will be buying them." She walked off to another car that had just arrived.

Another customer hurried over, flashlight beaming. "How much per hundred, Grandmother?"

"Eight baht."

"I'll take all you have. How many do you have?"

"Wait a minute, *Maekhaa*. You agreed to sell them to me!" the first woman said, pushing her way through anxiously. "She just sold these to me. I was the one who made the offer of eight baht per hundred just a minute ago. I had to go back to get a bag just now. Go and buy somewhere else."

The second woman turned away, looking disappointed. The original customer began counting the lemons as she dropped them into her bag. *Paa* Saaj looked on in silence.

"That's 1,000, with some left over, but still less than 100. So let's say an even 1,000. How about throwing in the rest for good measure to make up for those that are already rotting or damaged?"

Paa Saaj took the money, relieved and yet somehow sad at the same time. She piled her empty baskets on top of each other, hung them over her carrying pole, and wandered aimlessly about the market. She thought she might buy a few things to take home with her as soon as it grew lighter and she could see better.

The market was incredibly big. Kerosene lamps and candles flickered everywhere, as if vying with the stars in the heavens above. *Paa* Saaj peered at the faces of the market women, trying to find *Paa* Dii.

"Saaj, I'm over here. You've sold everything, have you?" It was *Paa* Dii, one hand carrying her baskets, the other holding a flashlight. She kept up her brisk pace without stopping.

"Yes, I've sold everything," *Paa* Saaj replied, trying to keep up with her friend.

"Good gracious, why were you in such a rush to sell everything? I went and reserved a space especially for you. So, how much did you get? And what about the limes?"

"Eight baht per hundred. It seemed a bit too cheap to me, but they bought all of them."

Paa Dii turned to look back for a moment. "Heavens, Saaj! Limes sell here for fifteen baht per hundred at the very least. We arrived here a little late. The merchant women from Chiang Mai had already arrived. You could have gotten twenty baht per hundred easily. If you're going to sell them that cheap, it's not worth all the trouble of coming to market. You let the middlemen take advantage of you!"

"What was that, Dii? Middle what?"

"The whole lot of them here. They buy cheap and sell dear, just like what happened to you. Everyone carrying flashlights, that's what all of them do. Even I hardly ever bring anything from home. I get it all around here. You just have to know how to talk well and how to buy. Villagers are stupid. Most of them don't come to sell goods, but usually to buy. But since they're coming anyway, they take the opportunity to bring whatever they might have to sell with them. Whatever we offer them, they sell for that. A little later, we resell it, this time for profit. Like your limes, they'll be selling for fifteen baht a hundred easily. If that woman takes them to sell in Chiang Mai, she'll get twenty to twenty–five baht for them. And if she goes herself and sits in the market in Chiang Mai, she'll be getting one baht for just two, three limes. Good profits with none of the tiring work of planting or picking."

"So if I were a marketseller in Chiang Mai, I could have gotten over 300 baht instead of just eighty for my limes?"

"No point in even thinking about escaping the middleman. To be a seller in the city market, you'd have to spend seventeen to eighteen baht a day on transportation. And more importantly, you'd need to have a pile of money to rent table space. The cheapest they go for is at least 1,500 baht per year. And there's no point in thinking of selling directly to the city marketsellers. They all have their regular buyers and sellers."

"So what should I do?"

"If you're thinking of doing any real buying and selling, be a middleman like me. Even though your own trees bear no limes, you'll still have limes to sell, and you can sell them for better profits than you'd get picking them yourself."

Bitterness and the Sold Water Buffalo

Joy had cared for many water buffaloes in his lifetime, but he had never loved any of them as much as *Ai* Ngaan. Father had bought *Ai* Ngaan to plow the paddyfields before they were planted with rice, just as he had bought all the other buffaloes. After the fields were plowed and readied for planting, Father would take them to the market to be sold, just as he had done year in and year out. But with the other buffaloes, Joy had never felt sad. In fact, he was glad that Father had sold them because then Joy no longer had to fetch grass and water to feed them.

"Father, do we have to sell *Ai* Ngaan?"

"Yes, son. Oxen and water buffaloes are hard to care for. There are so many thieves around. It's never certain when they might come and steal ours. As soon as the work of plowing is over, it's better to sell them. Keeping them just makes for needless worry."

"I'm sorry we have to sell him."

"I am, too. In all the time I have bought buffaloes, I have never bought one that pleased me as much as this one."

"I would like to keep this one and care for him. Father, will you let me keep him? Please don't sell him."

"Sorry, son. Last night *Lung* Phan's buffalo was stolen, even though it was tethered with a chain and locked up—even though *Lung* Phan was sleeping close by, guarding it. These days it's not as if buffaloes were cheap —they run 4,000 to 5,000 baht."

"So, how much will you sell him for, Father?"

"Well, we bought him for 4,500, so I'll try selling him for 5,000 baht."

"Are other buffaloes at market like *Ai* Ngaan, Father?"

"No, not the same. Would you like to go with me tomorrow? That way you can see for yourself."

"*Phii* Chom, it's so cold now and it's such a long way. I don't know what you were thinking about, asking the boy along as well. It would be better for him to stay home with me."

"No, Mother, I'd like to go."

"Let him go. We can come home by bus. Besides, I'll have him try on a new set of clothes."

Joy was awakened early in the morning while it was still dark. His mother urged him to hurry up, wash, and get dressed. Father was already wrapping food for breakfast in banana leaves and filling the bamboo containers with water to carry with them. When he saw Joy, he said gruffly, "Joy, last night *Lung* Sao's buffalo was stolen as well. We should hurry so we can go and come back quickly. Then maybe we could help the others track down the buffalo."

Joy was stunned. He understood why his father was rushing to sell *Ai* Ngaan. He could see from his father's movements that his father hadn't slept all night. If Father didn't sell the buffalo today, he probably wouldn't sleep well at night, having to guard and worry about *Ai* Ngaan every night for the remaining five or six months until the plowing season came again.

Joy put on all the clothing he had, layer upon layer, but he still felt cold. His mother helped him wrap a blanket around his shoulders and showed him how to pin it together with a safety pin. His father had already done the same. In the beam of the flashlight, Joy saw *Ai* Ngaan nearby, trembling in the cold.

"Are just the two of us going, Father?"

"Mmm. The others have gone to help search for *Lung* Sao's buffalo. They've found tracks heading west."

"Father, aren't you going to go and help them?"

"I'm going to help by having a look around the market. Generally though, they don't take newly stolen buffaloes to sell there."

By the time the man and his son arrived at the market, the day was just dawning. After tying *Ai* Ngaan beneath a *chamchaa* tree, they collected bits of wood and kindling to build a small fire to warm themselves.

"Be careful, Joy, you'll set your clothes on fire!"

"No one is coming, Father. How much longer until we finish the sale?"

"People are starting to come, but it's hard to see them clearly. The mist this morning is especially thick. The buyers will come after dawn, because, after all, it's not the plowing season."

"What difference does that make, Father?"

"If someone were buying a buffalo to plow his fields with, he would come very early in the morning like we did. The cattle that are being sold early in the morning belong to us villagers. But later in the day, the Burmese cattle from Mae Sarieng arrive and get mixed in with the rest, which makes it difficult to choose a good work animal. Can't tell anymore which animals can plow and which ones can't. And you can't trust the word of the cattle merchants."

"Father, if they aren't village buffaloes, does that mean you have to teach them how to plow?"

"That's right. Then we have to waste a lot more time training the buffalo. By the time the buffalo knows what to do, the time for plowing is nearly over. If you bought an untrained buffalo and then tried to sell it back, well, it would be difficult since the market is only held once a week."

Huge trucks arrived, one after the other in a long queue, making a noise that resounded through the entire market area. Once the truck motors finally fell silent, the shouts and lowing of cattle being whipped and herded rose up instead. Joy stood up and strained to see the cause of all the commotion through the morning mist. He could make out the dark grey masses of the buffaloes milling about. Father remained sitting silently by the fire warming himself, until finally two men wearing green military field–jackets came up.

"Hello, brother. You own this buffalo, do you? How much are you asking for him?"

"I would like to ask for about fifty."*

"It'll be hard to sell it at that price, brother. There are lots of buffaloes here today. How low will you go?"

"Fifty is already the cheapest possible price."

"I'll give you forty-one. Are you willing to sell for that?" the first man asked.

"Don't waste time bargaining with him. Let's hurry and go look in that area instead," the second man interrupted.

"I rather like this buffalo here."

"I don't think he's quite the right kind. He's a bit on the small side."

Joy quivered with rage at the second man. He was about to open his mouth to say something, but his father spoke first.

"He has just come from plowing the fields. If you let him rest, he'll fatten up. This buffalo is very strong and plows well. Look, sir, when he walks, the distance between the footprints of his hindlegs and his forelegs is only a hand's breadth apart.† If you aren't willing to pay fifty for him, I don't see that I can sell him."

"Will you take forty-two?" the man asked, looking his father straight in the eye while walking a full circle around *Ai* Ngaan. "I'll give you forty-two-and-a-half, that's my highest possible offer for this one."

Father shook his head and the two men walked off. Much later, lines of worry appeared on Father's face. Father took off the blanket he had been wearing and hung it over a tree branch. Joy did the same. Everywhere Joy looked, the unending mass of grey buffaloes intermingled with the indigo–blue shirts and

---

*Large sums of money are sometimes referred to in units of a hundred. Thus, fifty is fifty hundreds, or five thousand.

†The space between the hindlegs and forelegs of a water buffalo is important to Thai farmers as an indication of its agility in plowing. Villagers say a wide span suggests the animal is "lazy" and not good for field work.

white straw hats of the villagers; everything swam before his eyes. Many people came to bargain with Father, but all of them offered prices even lower than that of the first two men.

His father's eyes seem to brighten momentarily when he saw the first two men coming back again.

"So what's the decision? Will you sell for forty-two-and-a-half or not?"

"I'll come down to forty-five. I can't come down any lower than that. I'll be losing money otherwise. Honestly."

"Forty–three. I can't possible give you more than that."

"Alright. If forty-three is the offer, than forty-three it will have to be."

"Fine. In just a minute we'll arrange the bill of sale. I'll deposit one hundred baht with you first. Brother, wait here until then, alright? I must go and discuss arrangements with another two or three people and then we can all settle everything at the same time."

After a long while, the two men came back with a group of five or six people.

"So what do you think of this one? This is the one I was telling you about just a second ago." The one man spoke as he led *Ai* Ngaan back and forth expertly.

"Agreed? It's the best looking in the market. Five thousand is a very reasonable price."

"Agreed," a man in the group of five or six men answered, evidently well satisfied.

*   *   *

"Father, Father, why did we only get 4,300? I saw those men paying 5,000 baht for *Ai* Ngaan, didn't you see?"

"I saw. Why wouldn't I have seen that? But the other 700 baht are for the two go-betweens and the registration cost of the bill of sale."

"So how much did the two go-betweens get, Father?"

"Six hundred plus. The two will split that between them, so each will get about 300 baht."

"So why did you let them, why?"

"That was the price we agreed on, my son. Agents are clever. They know who are regulars and who are newcomers, who must sell and who is serious about buying. We have no way of winning over them."

"But you lost 200 baht."

"Never mind, son. It doesn't matter. Just look at it as having been the price of renting a buffalo for the season. And 200 baht is still a lot cheaper than the real cost of renting a buffalo."

Dividing the Rice

"I think back on all the years I have been farming. When will the day come when I will once have enough money to afford to build a house of wood?"

Lung Mii raised the last bundle of ricestalks high above his head and beat it down on the ground with all his might. He gently released the bundle from between the wood pincers and tossed the bundle on top of the gigantic mound of threshed ricestalks nearby. He then walked over and sat down cross–legged with the group of five or six men who had been waiting for him to finish.

"If you got a heap of rice this size every year, you'd live comfortably for a long time. But only half of all this rice will be left for you by tomorrow," said one of the seated men, while handing *Lung* Mii a glass of village liquor.

"Right! Every year the landowners take half our crops. If we plant rice, they take rice. If we plant soybeans, they take soybeans. If we plant garlic or onions, they take that as well," another man added.

"According to my father, *Ai* Suk inherited this plot of land from his father, who acquired this plot of land by simply exchanging a basket of *miang** for it."

"The land adjoining this plot that now belongs to *Ai* Nuay was originally just given free to *Ai* Nuay's father by some ranking official or lord. His father seemed to have some kind of title."

"But *Ai* Sao, whose land I am now renting, actually bought that plot of land with his own savings, didn't he?"

"No, *Ai* Ryan, not so. Originally that land belonged to *Ai* Maa, but then *Ai* Maa borrowed money from *Ai* Saw. When *Ai* Maa couldn't meet the interest payments, he had to sell his land instead."

"So has any landlord acquired his land respectably?"

"Only a few. And almost none of them let someone work their land for nothing. In our village, the only people I can think of are *Ai* Jan, *Ai* Saeng, and *Ai* Kham."

Miang is a kind of fermented tea leaf that is very popular in northern Thailand. It is eaten after meals, usually chewed with a small piece of salt.

"Which *Ai* Kham?" a voice interrupted.

"Kham Yao."

"Oh, I thought you meant Kham, *Ee* Phuang's husband."

The mention of the pitiable man who struggled to make his living catching fish in the paddyfields brought peals of laughter. *Lung* Mii became angry. "It's not right to make fun of people worse off than ourselves!"

Everyone grew quiet. *Lung* Mii escaped the long hush by going over to the lantern that was hanging nearby and pumping it full of air. Finally the youngest member of the group broke the stillness, speaking in a serious tone, "Do you know about what's been happening in Mae Waeng village?"

"I heard the village headman's son was shot and nearly killed. Something to do with the FFT,[*] PFT, or whatever it's called. If you know something about the incident, tell us."

"*Ai* Song, the one who was shot, is a close friend of mine, but never mind that. But do you know how they divide the rice with the landlords in Mae Waeng? Ever since last year, the landlords only get one-third of the rice harvest."

"So I've heard. They say they're following the law. But that law is for big landlords."

"No, it's not. The law doesn't stipulate only the big landlords; it covers all landholders, regardless how much land they own. And all tenants, regardless how many *rai* they rent."

"Just what does the law say?"

"*Ai* Song told me the law says to divide the rice into three parts. One-third is to cover the labor and expenses in planting; the tenant and the landowner then each get one-third to keep."

"So the landlord really only gets one-third?"

"Exactly. And furthermore, if we plant a second or third crop after the rice is harvested, the landowner has no right to claim any portion of those crops."

"But what landlord is going to be willing to agree to that? Law may be law, but since when does that mean anything? Just look at what happens when we borrow money from *Ai* Sao. *Ai* Sao writes in the agreement that the interest

---

[*]The Farmers Federation of Thailand (FFT) was founded on November 19, 1974. This movement, particularly strong in northern Thailand, petitioned the government for land reform. When the government passed the Land Rent Control Act in November 1974, the movement tried to encourage tenant farmers to take advantage of the law, which led to tremendous conflicts and the murder of farmer leaders. At the time this story was written, over twenty FFT leaders had been assassinated, most of them in the north. This story provides important background information as to the reasons for the conflict. For more information about the general context of the period, see the Introduction.

charged will be in accordance with the law.* And then he turns around and charges the going rate of five percent a month."

"Uncle, let me finish what I'm saying. The law forces landowners to let us rent their land for a minimum of another six years. After that, if they want to end the agreement, they cannot just do so at will."

"And what if they don't agree?"

"We can bring the case to court, the maximum sentence being a prison term of six months. And there are various groups who will support us, like the students and the Farmers Federation. If you want, I can contact those groups for you."

"You mean you think we should try following the law?"

"Exactly! What are we all waiting for? The law was passed last year. How long have they been allowed to exploit us already?"

"Let *Ai* Mii try it first. He has to divide his rice tomorrow. What about it, Ai Mii? You've been grumbling about wanting to build a wood house with a tin roof, haven't you?"

"Alright, I'll try talking to him. But is everyone else just going to talk and not do anything? Anyone else going to give it a try? For this to get anywhere, we must be united. Isn't everyone else here a tenant farmer, too?"

"If you do it, I'll go in as well."

"Me, too."

"So will I."

"Fine. So we'll all try talking it over with our landowners and see if there are any problems. It's about time they started sympathizing with our problems a bit more. As it is, we're all so poor that we barely get enough rice to eat."

"So when should we meet again?"

"How about at *Ai* Kyyt's the day after tomorrow? That's when he's planning to thresh his rice. And that would leave tomorrow free for each of us to talk things over with our own landowners."

"Fine. It's already too late tonight, so we might as well split up and go home. I'm going now. Goodnight everyone. *Ai* Mii, good luck tomorrow. Why didn't you tell your wife to come and sleep here with you tonight to help guard the rice?"

On the appointed day, the sun was barely rising over *Lung* Kyyt's paddyfields. The dew was just beginning to dry. But the men who were to help each other thresh the rice had all arrived long before.

"*Ai* Som isn't coming?"

"He went into town and isn't back yet. He'll be back this evening."

---

*Not over 15 percent per year.

"So, *Ai* Mii, what happened? Anything come out of it?" one of the last to arrive pressed.

"*Ai* Suk said if he was only going to get one–third of the rice, then he'd be better off hiring wage labor on a day-by-day basis. If I were really only going to give him one–third, he'd agree to it, but after the six years were up, he'd take the land back."

"I didn't get anywhere either. *Ai* Nuay said that even dividing the rice in half, as we have been doing, he is losing money."

"How is he losing money?"

"He said if he sold his paddyfields, he'd get 8,000 baht per rai. If he put that money in the bank, he would get 640 baht in interest a year. Now, he gets at most forty to fifty *thang** from renting his land out. With rice selling at twenty baht per *thang*, he gets less than 600 baht per *rai*. If he were to agree to only getting one–third, he would keep his land for at most another year before selling it."

"*Ai* Sao said exactly what *Ai* Nuay said, except that he said he would sell the land and use the money to lend out to other people. Lending out the money he would get from one rai, he would earn interest of not under 400 baht per month. What's worse, he wanted to let me keep only one–third!"

"*Ai* Kham spoke much more kindly than the others seem to have."

"What did he say?"

"He said that when he had dug up the land and made it into paddyfields, I hadn't helped him shovel one load of dirt. He said that it hadn't been easy to terrace the land so the top section was higher than the rest, so that the water from the irrigation streams would flow properly and fill every terrace evenly. He wouldn't be able to begin to count how many shovelfuls of dirt it had taken, let alone all the time he had spent doing it. But if he collected the sweat that had poured off his body in the process, it would flow from the uppermost terrace all the way down to the lowest one. The only reason he is letting me work his land is out of compassion. He saw that I couldn't find steady work anywhere. But that if I didn't have sympathy for his position as well, then I should return his land. He spoke much more eloquently than I just did, much more. He spoke so movingly that I wept."

"So, in conclusion, it seems none of us got anywhere.

"Sure we did. But when 1980 comes, we want to still be farming."

"So that's the way it stands. There doesn't seem much point in discussing it anymore. We might as well get going."

---

* A *thang* contains 20 liters of rice or 10 kilograms.

Lung Mii stood up as he spoke and walked over to the mound of newly harvested rice. Binding a bundle between his wooden pincers, he walked over to the
edge of the dung-caked threshing ground.*

"Hey, there they are, landlords' heads! Let's thrash them!"†

"Thrash what?"

"Thrash the rice!"**

And as the sun rose higher in the morning sky, the villagers who had come
to help each other thresh *Lung* Kyyt's rice were all hard at work slamming rice
stalks against the ground, the sweat of their bodies silently darkening their blue
shirts.††

---

*Surasingh added this paragraph to the story after it was published in *Jaturat* and made the addition available to the translator in 1978.

†This is a reference to a well-known game played by village children. If there were someone they
hated or were angry with, they would mark a circle on the ground representing their enemy's head
and stomp it with their feet until their frustration had dissipated. In this case, the threshing ground
has been designated as the landlords' heads.

**The author is making a pun. *Tii* means to "beat, hit, thrash, or thresh," as in beating a person
or beating the rice.

††This paragraph was added to the published version by Surasingh and made available to the
translator in 1978.

The Fount of Compassion

"Phrim, you're home already! It's so soon! So, what did the doctor say?"

"Mother was right! So now we've spent over 200 baht, with busfare, food, and medicine. Ahh, I feel so tired. Waiting half the day to get the hospital registration card, then to see the doctor—all for a little bit of medicine that will be gone in just a couple days."

"It's not as if I didn't tell you so. But neither of you would listen to me. Trying to act like you know everything better than anyone else, trying to be in fashion. Spending money offering sacrifices to the spirits was quite sufficient, but you had to waste even more time and money going to see a doctor. Since when did you suddenly get so rich? *Ai* Dam's ghost with the iron hand, that's what it was! His power is notorious. Everyone around here knows that. The people he strikes fall sick without fail."

"Mother, * I believe you. Why wouldn't I? If I didn't believe you, would I have been willing offer sacrifices to the spirits? I just want Phrim to get better quickly."

"You can't expect to get better from one day to the next, not even if the gods treated you. But your doctor gave great advice—rest a lot. Great help that is! As if there were no work to be done around the house—no need to earn money selling things at the market. Fine, eat good food. Finding any kind of food, just to make the stomach feel full, is already beyond ..."

"That's enough, Mother. Pan is tired from working all day. We can talk about all this later. Husband, I brought some noodles back for you. They're in the kitchen. We can eat them with the rice tonight, but, of course, the children will decide they have first rights to the meatballs."

"Phrim, that was kind of you. But let's wait and eat together. So, how many days should you rest? I'll go and ask my younger sister to come and help with the housework. The children are still too small to be able to fetch water."

---

*Thai village residence patterns are generally matrilocal and frequently consist of extended rather than nuclear families; in this context, the husband marrying into the wife's family also addresses the wife's mother as "Mother."

"That's not necessary, Pan. Mother can help with some of the lighter tasks. But I am worried about not going to the market. If I don't go, other sellers will take over my regular customers. I think I'll stay home and rest for a few days. Then I'll go to the market. If you could perhaps carry the baskets there. Then I wouldn't have any physical work to do—it'd be just the same as staying home to rest."

*   *   *

"Phrim, it's already late. Go to bed and sleep. I can take care of what is left to be done. Everything should be cooked soon, and I'll get everything arranged and put it in the baskets for you."

"Thanks, Pan, but I couldn't sleep yet anyhow. I'm not tired. Could you bring in some more firewood."

Pan laid the coconut shell he had just scraped clean next to the tray. He took a kerosene lamp with him, went down the stairs to gather firewood, and piled an armful next to the stove. Then he sat down where he had been sitting before. He picked up a coconut shell and examined it with satisfaction. Its shape was perfect for making a beautiful water ladle. One had to wait a long time to find a shell that was as beautifully shaped. Pan determined to make an elegant handle for it. Then they would sell it for more than the two baht they were usually paid.

Tonight, like the previous two or three nights, Pan had had to stop making ladles to help Phrim make sweets. The coconut shells, already boiled, had been allowed to accumulate so that now they more than filled the large clay pot. But however much he wanted to finish off those ladles, when he saw Phrim's face, Pan wanted to do everything for her. Even though his mother–in–law was doing even more than she was really capable of at her age, she lightened Phrim's load only a little. The doctor's words, "rest a lot," tormented Pan.

Pan often felt bitter than he had been born "without even a small field to his name." Even the land on which his bamboo hut was built belonged to his mother–in–law. Without land, he had no right to be a "farmer," now that farmers were getting paid so much attention.[*] He was merely a worker in a small factory earning twenty baht a day for his labor, even less than Phrim earned some days. But it was good that at least he also had coconut ladles to sell—it helped.

Pan looked up to remind Phrim once more than it was getting late, before putting his own things away. The wood from the small stove flickered, illuminating Phrim's pale wan face. He sighed with fear, and he felt a sadness he could

---

[*]During the period of the mid-1970s, the civilian government focussed considerable attention on the farmers, as did student and other activist organizations. Very little attention was paid towards the rural proletariat or landless poor.

not put into words. Phrim was only twenty-four years old, but she looked even older than the middle–aged society ladies who had come to the village to distribute blankets.[*]

Phrim continued going to bed late and getting up early; not many days later, she fell ill again with the same symptoms. She complained of general aches and pains, but especially in her neck, shoulders, and back. However her mother massaged her, the aches would not disappear. She took pain relievers costing twenty-five *satang* a package. If she only had aches and pains, that would have been all right; but she also felt dizzy, and her hands and feet trembled, her eyes burned, and her ears felt stuffy.

Phrim was at her wits' end. It was beyond her means to keep buying medicines indefinitely. She had offered sacrifices to the spirits. She had been to the hospital. The only avenue she hadn't tried yet was what the local monk, Intha, had suggested: that she should go and see the abbot at Thung Luang Temple.

With the money Pan was able to get as an advance from work and some borrowed in Phrim's name from other women selling at the market, the trip of over one hundred kilometers to Thung Luang Temple passed comfortably. The cost of transportation had not been expensive, since they hadn't had to hire special transportation. For the two of them, Phrim and her mother, the journey came to fifty baht.

The temple was relatively free of people milling about. The driver of the mini–bus explained that when the abbot used to give free medical treatment, people came in such swarms that they virtually blackened the land. Cars were parked kilometers away from the temple. Sick people would have to stop to rest several times before finally reaching the temple, and then have to wait one or two days before being able to see the abbot for treatment. But now it had become difficult to find the necessary herbs, so the temple committee had to charge fees. Now the people who were not really sick didn't come and bother the abbot anymore.

*　　*　　*

"You've come to see the abbot, have you? Please come this way. He happens to be free at the moment."

Phrim meekly followed the man as instructed. Prim's mother carried a bundle of clothing with her. When the two arrived, they knelt down and prostrated themselves before the abbot three times, as was the custom.

---

[*]The phrase used in the text is *khunying*. In the past *khunying* referred to members of the aristocracy, but today the phrase is used for high-society women in general.

"Welcome and be blessed. So, have you been sick for long? Tell me the number of years, months, and days."

"I've been sick off and on for two years, five months, and twenty-three days before coming here. Ever since my father died."

"Have you been making merit on his behalf?"

"Yes. I give to beggars, put rice and food into the monks' bowls, and I contribute money to the temples on festival days. Unfortunately, I haven't been able to go to the temples myself to make merit. I have no free time in the mornings as I have to go to the market."

"What! That's no way to make merit on your father's behalf. To make merit for a deceased person, you must go to the temple and have the blessed lustral water poured on the ground. The Pali texts tell of a man named Manop who, without fail, upon his father's death, crossed a bridge in order to make food offerings at the site where his father died. One day the bridge was destroyed, so Manop couldn't take the food across the bridge. But then suddenly monks in yellow robes appeared, so he took the food and offered it to the monks, explaining his reason at the same time. The monks then took lustral water and poured it onto the ground for the father of Manop.

"That night, Manop dreamt that his father came to him to thank him, but also reproached him saying that he had been dead such a long time already and why only now had he thought to make merit? That was when Manop learned that when he had been offering food at the site where his father died, only the birds, mice, dogs, crows, chickens, and destitute beggars benefited. It didn't reach his father as lustral water hadn't been poured on the ground by the monks as had been done that one morning."

The abbot went on preaching and questioning Phrim in further detail. Phrim answered listlessly, much like a robot. She came to life only when the abbot had a small piece of paper placed before her.

PATIENT IDENTIFICATION

Card No. 3135   Thung Luang Temple

Name: Mrs. Phrim Khohnkaew.

Residence: Dohnton Village, Huay Yao Tambon,
Phrao District, Chiang Mai Province.

Diagnosis: Suffering from supernatural forces, primarily caused by not having made merit on behalf of her deceased father. This has resulted in the present illness, boil of cancer. Numbing winds entered the joints causing weakness, swelling, aches in the small of the back, the back and the base of the neck, in turn resulting in sleeplessness, trembling hands and feet and occasional dizzy spells for a period of 2 years, 5 months, and 23 days. The prescribed period of steaming in herbs at the temple is 24 days, together with worship and herbal medicines to cure the illness. The cost of the steaming and other medicines is 363 baht.

(Signed) Abbot Buntham
The Fount of Compassion.

Phrim read for such a long time that the abbot felt edgy. He worried that Phrim perhaps did not know how to read.

"Pay the 363 baht here, and in a moment I'll have a temple committee member take you to your quarters. Women must sleep in the shelter outside the temple grounds. Getting food here is no problem. Market vendors come selling here regularly. But before eating, please note the instructions written on the back."

Phrim swallowed, feeling the moisture pass down the back of her throat when she saw her mother counting the money to give to the abbot. Phrim turned the card over and read on the back:

FORBIDDEN. Do not consume: *namwaa* bananas, pickled fish, crabsauce, ox–meat, pickled garlic, *waen* and *cha–om* vegetables, *duk* fish, and tobacco for the rest of your life.

Phrim was stunned. How could she possibly avoid these forbidden foods? They were the staple foods of any villager, especially poor villagers. Of all bananas, *namwaa* bananas are the cheapest and most available; every villager grows up with them. Just twenty-five *satang* of pickled fish mixed with chili was enough for her family to eat with rice for a day. *Waen* and *cha–om* are among the cheapest vegetables, especially *waen*—she and her children often gathered it from the paddyfields where it grew in abundance. Similarly she and her children would catch crabs from the paddyfields every year to make into crab sauce to use as flavoring throughout the rest of the year; a half tablespoon of crab-sauce mixed with chili comprised one of the dishes her family frequently ate with their rice. Only rich people could hope to be able to avoid those foods. She sat silently, her thoughts in a quandary, until a man came to bring her to

She sat silently, her thoughts in a quandary, until a man came to bring her to her quarters.*

*   *   *

"Did you get better, Phrim? You were gone so long. I wanted to visit you, but I had to work."

"I'm all better. You've made so many ladles! Tomorrow I'll take them to sell for you."

"Good heavens, Phrim, don't start worrying about going to market so quickly. What was the abbot's treatment like?"

"To steam in herbs two or three times and eat medicine made of boiled herbs. Other than that, nothing much. I just slept and did nothing. I really want to get back to the market."

"Phrim, do you suppose that if you stayed and rested at home for twenty or thirty days, it might have had the same effect as going to sleep in the temple? You might have got better just the same."

"I feel like you do, Pan. But the good thing about going to the temple is that you make merit at the same time. We are poor. If we don't make merit, what hope is there for us?"

---

*Surasingh added this paragraph to the story text as it appeared in *Jaturat* after it was published, to ensure that the urban and/or Western reader would understand the significance of the prohibition against eating these particular foods. This expanded text was made available to the translator by the author in 1978.

Burmese Buddha Images

"That's why Burma is going to wrack and ruin—even the Buddha images and Buddhism itself are fleeing to Ayothaya.* Sometimes they are disappearing in three, four truckloads at a time."

Bunryang was amused by the elderly lady's simplistic, albeit sincere, lament on the trade in Burmese Buddha images. It was an old-fashioned idea that nearly everyone of his generation had long since stopped believing.

"Nephew, buying and selling Buddha images is not right. The demerit you will bring upon yourself will destroy you. Buddha images aren't sold. If someone wants a Buddha image to worship, they rent them. Images are rented, not sold."†

Bunryang had to restrain a desire to laugh outright when he heard these words. But then it suddenly dawned on him that what she was saying had been true. In the days of *Mae Thao* Saeng Ching, Buddha images had not been sold. In her day, it was hardly ever necessary to use money. Even when they had some money, they didn't know what to spend it on, except to make merit and build temples for their children to play in, to be ordained in, to study the Dharma, or whatever. But for him, in his present situation, he had four children, each of whom needed an article or two of clothing.

Mae Thao Saeng Ching saw that Bunryang had fallen silent, so she stopped talking. Instead she reached for her mortar and pestle and busied herself filling it with betel nut and other ingredients. The mortar was only made of brass, but it shone luminously from frequent use. The betel tray was simply made, like those of other villagers, the decorative patterns formed by the interweaving of

---

*Ayothaya is a term sometimes used by old people to refer to Bangkok, stemming from the days when the capital of Thailand was in the city presently called Ayutthaya.

†Since monks are forbidden to be concerned directly with money and since Buddhism teaches that the concept of ownership is a false attachment to property, a paradox arises with the sale and ownership of Buddha images. originally Buddha images were kept only in the temples, which belong to the village community at large. Since those days, a commercial market in the private ownership of Buddha images has arisen, but propriety disguises the fact of the buying and selling of Buddha images in a linguistic nicety of *chao*, or "renting."

the lighter colored bamboo flesh and the darker colored bamboo skin. Day by day, she took pleasure in her few possessions—her betel nut tray, a box filled with tobacco and dried leaf wrappers for rolling cigars, a tin enamel plate with salt and miang wrapped up on top of it, a clay water pitcher, a mat and pillows lying about on the raised platform under her house. She was the only Shan[*] in this town that Bunryang knew well, and then only because she had been married to his uncle who had died two or three years ago.

Before coming to see *Mae Thao* Saeng Ching in Mae Hong Sorn province, Bunryang and his friends had sold their rice and garlic crops at prices with which they were less than satisfied. In the hope of beginning a better life than they had had before, Bunryang and four of his friends had decided to pool their money. They had raised amongst themselves a total of 25,000 baht with which to trade in Burmese Buddha images. These art objects had already enabled several of their friends in the village to rapidly improve their financial position within the past year. After learning the trade routes from previous buyers, his friends had entrusted the matter to Bunryang, to proceed alone in order to cut down on expenses. The decision to invest their money on this occasion meant that if they lost the money, they wouldn't have enough to eat until the next harvest.

Mae Thao Saeng Ching's son made it possible for Bunryang to meet Khinnu in the village of Nara–Orn without difficulty. Khinnu was a middle–aged woman, strong–willed, capable, and efficient. Had *Mae Thao* Saeng Ching's son not told him, Bunryang would not have suspected in the least that she and others like her had travelled alone as far as Bangkok selling Burmese Buddhas. Khinnu spoke several languages, including English. Her husband was a soldier.[†] Once in a long while he would return home, but women like Khinnu didn't need anyone to take care of them. After visiting, her husband often left home with large amounts of money that Khinnu had made.

Nara–Orn was such a small village that it didn't seem possible that it could have anything for sale, but as Khinnu stated succinctly, "All roads lead to Nara–Orn." Nara–Orn had a variety of articles that could be sold in Chiang Mai for at least twice the original price: antiques such as carved wooden Buddha figures, painted red with gold leaf and inset with colored glass. These could be bought for 1,000 baht per *sokh*[**] and resold for 2-3,000 baht. Pleated manuscript books embellished with gold and colored lacquer could be

---

[*] The Shans are a sub-group of the T'ai peoples, living along the borders of northwestern Thailand, northeastern Burma, particularly in the Shan Staates, and in southern China.

[†] There were various Shan resistance movements fighting against the Burmese government.

[**] A *sokh* is the distance between the tip of one hand and elbow, or equivalent to 50 centimeters.

6,000 baht each could be sold for over twice that amount. These were just some of the many items that were hidden under scattered piles of leaves and branches in the forest surrounding the village.

Bunryang wanted to buy everything he saw. Khinnu had to help him with the selection and had to remind him to save 4,000 baht to get across the border. Khinnu took the 4,000 baht and divided it between three envelopes, numbering each of them. The first envelope had the most money. Bunryang complained that it was a shame to waste this money. Khinnu had to explain that with the small amount of capital that he had, it almost wasn't worth getting involved in this business, since the money might not be enough to cover the "taxes" that he would be charged at each of the checkpoints he passed.

Bunryang left Baan Nara-Orn feeling a deep debt of gratitude to Khinnu. She had even taken the trouble to escort him to the border. By that time the passenger buses had stopped running. There remained only lorries whose drivers didn't mind picking up passengers, who in turn were willing to endure the discomfort. Once settled in the truck, Bunryang couldn't restrain himself from happily visualizing the future he had been dreaming about.

Bunryang passed the various checkpoints until he no longer had any envelopes. Going through the jungle was frightening, both sides of the road dark and murky. The front headlights of the truck beamed forward, chasing away the darkness bit by bit. Many times brown rabbits came out of the jungle, hopped playfully in and out of the headlight beams, and then disappeared into the jungle alongside the road again.

All of a sudden a small red light of a flashlight blinked in the darkness in front of the truck. The truck came to a stop. A group of young men dressed in green and yellow camouflage uniforms, bristling with weapons, ran up to the truck with flashlights. A voice questioned the driver gently, "*Phiichaaj,* do you have anything with you on this trip?"

"Nothing much. All are goods on which duties have already been paid," the driver replied.

"What's in this bag here that's so heavy?"

"Burmese Buddha images. We have only a few with us."

"Whose are they?"

"Mine," Bunryang answered.

"Oh, good evening, Patron. So, you got some beautiful things on this trip, did you? If you had come just a bit sooner, it would have been easier to find things like this. Two or three days ago though they were transporting them by the truckload. With things like these you can make a lot of money."

Bunryang nodded his head in agreement, but suddenly felt a chill run down his spine.

"So, Patron, how about giving us some money to buy a little liquor. There are six or seven of us. We'll settle for a bottle of *Maekhong** each. Or even better, a few bottles of soda and some snack foods to eat with it," he said laughing at the same time.

Bunryang felt his mouth and throat trembling. "I ... I have no money left. I used it all up in buying the Buddha images and paying the checkpoint fees. Could I be allowed to pay you on my next trip, sir?"

"Fellows! This character here is acting suspiciously. He's probably one of the gang transporting heroin that the intelligence people alerted us to this morning."

"Mmm, seems likely. Better check to see. Unload one or two of these bags and search it."

Bunryang was nervous, but also pleasantly relieved that he wasn't transporting any heroin.

"Certainly. Please feel free to examine everything for yourselves, sir."

Flashlights shone to and fro, finally settling on one particular Buddha statue. The light caught one of the pieces of colored glass, beautiful to behold, yet terrifying.

"I bet it's hidden in this statue. These types like to hide things in Buddha images and then cover it over with these bits of glass. Bring me the axe."

Bunryang was shocked. When he saw the arm bearing the axe raised high about to strike, he cried out to stop them, his voice shrill, "Don't! Please don't! Sir, please, I beg of you! There is really nothing inside. I swear, sir, there is nothing."

"Seize him! We have to make sure. Even if he hasn't done it, his Burmese buddies may have hidden some, thinking to buy it back at the other end of the journey."

The crash of the axe hitting the glass mirrors and wood was agony for Bunryang. It also caused shudders deep in the hearts of the truck driver and the other four or five passengers who were standing about, watching in silence.

The Buddha statue was a reclining Buddha two *sohk* in length. Khinnu had given it to him at a special price of 2,000 baht. It was the most intact of all her Buddhas, and she had been keeping it for a long time, reluctant to let it go. "For the nephew of *Mae Thao* Saeng Ching," Khinnu had said. "You will be able to sell this in Chiang Mai for no less than 6,000 baht."

The axe eventually fell silent, but the pain seared unabated. The voice speaking seemed to come from somewhere in the far distance, "Well, that statue did-

---

*Maekhong, produced under a government monopoly contract, is one of the best known and, by village standards of the day, most expensive Thai liquors.

The axe eventually fell silent, but the pain seared unabated. The voice speaking seemed to come from somewhere in the far distance, "Well, that statue didn't have any. Let's try another one or two."

Bunryang felt weak and weary. Tears welled up silently, his thoughts in confusion. *Mae Thao* Saeng Ching was right. But he wanted to tell *Mae Thao* that it wasn't the Buddha images that had brought about his ruin, that had sold him into destitution this time. And it wasn't his fault, nor the fault of Khinnu, in the least.

It would not be difficult for Bunryang to explain what had happened to *Mae Thao* Saeng Ching, or his friends and wife.

But it would take a long time for his four children to understand.

Amphorn's New Hope

"Amphorn, you're an excellent student—you always place first. I'd like you to continue on to the fifth grade. Our school is going to begin teaching fifth grade next year. You would be a member of our first class if you kept on. You'd be a credit to our school. If you like, I will help discuss the matter with your mother and father."

The words of Teacher Saen weighed heavily on Amphorn's mind. She wanted to be able to study further. She wanted to become a teacher. Her parents also wanted her to get an education so she could became a government official.* But when the school term finished, her parents had asked her to work to earn the money to pay for her books and supplies.

So now a huge building made of plain uncoated bricks rose up in front of her. Imposing and intimidating, it was not like a school building. School buildings have lots of doors and windows. She could still recall her nervousness when she had entered the school building that first day.

Amphorn felt afraid. She scolded herself for coming late. But she had lost time consoling her younger brother when she dropped him off with *Paa* Phen, who ran a village day care center. Every time she had tried to leave, he had come running after her. If it hadn't been for that, she wouldn't have come so late and could have gone into the enormous building with friends.

She was able to open the tin door just wide enough to slip by. The eyes of all the girls sitting scattered here and there behind piles of dried leaves turned to look at her. Amphorn was nervous, but was reassured when she heard the voices of everyone greeting her at once.

"*Ee* Phorn."

"So you, too, have come to work sorting tobacco leaves, have you? Come on over here and sit next to me. You can come and help me sort first if you like. Once you know how to do it, then you can go and do it by yourself."

---

*The Thai word for government official used in the text is *jaokhon naikhon*, which translates literally as "lord of people, master of people." Today a less laden tern is *khaa ratchakaan*, which, literally translated, is "servant of the king." For the majority of Thai villagers, the jobs of teacher and policeman are the most sought-after government positions.

The girl who had been talking to her slid over and eagerly dusted off a space for Amphorn. Amphorn sank down onto the cement floor; she put her little lunchbag beside her. All of a sudden she felt the stifling heat and humidity of the air inside the building. No matter where she turned to look, there wasn't a single window. There didn't even appear to be a crack for a breeze to squeeze through. The smell of the tobacco burned in her nose. Perspiration oozed until her body was drowning in it.

"It's really hot and stuffy in here."

"Don't complain. There's no need to complain. It seems hot when you first come in, but after a while you get used to it. The factory doesn't allow open windows or doors. The fresh air would dry out the tobacco leaves and it would lose its price."

"Do you know how to sort? No, no, not like that! What are you doing holding the stick that way? Don't hold the sharp end of the threading stick towards you. You're terrifying me doing that! Ah, that's right, hold it sideways. Ah my, if I spend all day having to teach you, how many kilos will I be able to get done today?* Even worse, now there are only these light–weight leaves left to sort."

"Tobacco like this is easy to sort, but each kilo takes a long time. You should separate the leaves into three piles. Put the large leaves in one place, the middle-sized leaves in another pile, and the small leaves in a third pile. Leaves like this they call sugar–brown. If you see tobacco leaves of any other color than this, stack them separately. They may have disease flecks, or be too yellow, or so dry they look red. I'll tell you how to sort those another day."

Amphorn carefully began pulling threaded tobacco off of the sharp–ended two-foot-long bamboo sticks. The sugar–brown leaves stuck together in sheets. Amphorn's small hands separated the leaves one by one and cautiously made separate piles. Initially clumsy and awkward, she soon become more and more adept. The pile of sorted leaves grew bigger and bigger, until it was time to stop for lunch. The workers broke into small groups as they left the sorting building, greeting friends, inviting them to eat lunch together, and chattering happily as they waited for fellow workers who were still engrossed in their work.

"So Phorn, how is it? Is your new job fun? How many kilos do you plan to get done today? Why don't you stop to eat though?"

Amphorn smiled in embarrassment, nodding her head in agreement as she picked up her lunchbag and followed the others out. No sooner had she passed through the door than she felt chilled, even though the hot midday April sun was beating down. But when the sweat had dried, the burning heat replaced the chill. As she washed her face and hands, her friends crowded around her greeting her and inviting her to join them eating lunch under the shade of a coconut

---

*Workers are paid on a piece-work basis, according to the number of kilos they sort.

greeting her and inviting her to join them eating lunch under the shade of a coconut tree.

"So your teachers want you to keep on with your studies, isn't that right, Phorn? But, however well you do, you won't forget all of us working here, will you?

"Of course not. But what about you? Aren't you going to go on, too? Next year they're going to begin teaching fifth grade in our village. We won't have to travel all the way to the district town to school anymore."

"No, I'm not going to school again. It's a blessing that I finished what I did. If I went on and then failed the exam, all that time would have just been wasted for nothing."

"They're also going to begin teaching secondary school in our village soon, aren't they?"

"Not likely. Look at any village anywhere—they all only teach up to grade seven. If you want to go to secondary school, you still have to go to the district town or provincial capital."

"Phorn, are you going to be able to travel all that way? All the way to the district town? You'll have to pay bus fare. And even then, the district school only goes up to grade ten."

"*Phii* Phit is right. If you only study up to grade ten and then quit, you still can't get any sort of job. You'd still have to go on then to the provincial capital."

And when you've finished in the capital, then you'd have to go on to Bangkok or another big province. Just look at *Phii* Kaew, the *kamnan's* daughter—look what happened to her.* Even now, she still hasn't found a job."

My father once told me that *Phii* Kaew is already twenty-two or twenty-three years old. And she still hasn't brought home a single baht yet."

"How far did *Phii* Kaew study? Anyone know?"

"My father said she finished a teaching diploma, but that she can't teach at the village school because she studied too high and is over–qualified. She can only get a teaching job at the district or provincial schools. But her father doesn't want her to go so far away from home because she is his only daughter."†

"Then why did he let his daughter study so long in the city? I bet they're lying. I've heard that lots of people with fancy educations can't find work."

"Phorn, what would you like to be?"

---

*A *kamnan* is the head of a tambon, or sub-district. A *tambon* is an administrative unit comprised of many villages, each village headed by a village headman. The *kamnan* is a village headman, who has also been locally elected to serve as *tambon* head. The *kamnan* is generally chosen from among the wealthiest members of the community.

†In Thai society, the youngest daughter traditionally inherits the family house and an extra portion of land with which to care for the parents in their old age. Parents with only one daughter are extremely concerned not to have her move away.

"Phorn, what would you like to be?"

"I still don't know, *Phii* Phit. I'd really like to be a teacher, but I don't know if I can study that far."

"You probably can. You're a clever student. And your father is a carpenter, so he must earn at least fifty baht a day."

"But, *Phii* Phit, that's just it. If no one hires him, my father has no work and then he doesn't earn a single baht. You know that there aren't many who can hire him. In one year, he has at most only three, four months of work. Father keeps saying that if we lived in the city, he'd have work all year round, but he doesn't like living in the city."

The sound of a bell announced the beginning of the afternoon. The air inside the sorting building was even stuffier, hotter, and more humid than before. But no one complained. Everyone went back to their old places and diligently set to work. The tobacco leaves passed those small hands endlessly as they were sorted out into different piles. Her eyes swam. The afternoon heat invited sleep. Amphorn was thinking about the comments of her friends; they made her feel unhappy. She'd have to study another eight years before she could finally become a teacher like Teacher Saen. Everyone thought her father was rich, but Amphorn knew her family was poor. Her mother and father both had to hire themselves out as construction workers in the city. Between the two of them they earned one hundred baht a day, after deducting transportation costs.

Amphorn had seen her parents short of money time and time again. Each time, her mother and father had had long, sad faces, especially during the rainy season when they couldn't find construction work. Then they had to gather vegetables and catch fish, or work as hired laborers in the paddyfields, depending on what work was available. And every time Amphorn had opened her mouth to ask for money to buy needed school supplies, her mother would look heavy-hearted.

Amphorn was totally engrossed in her thoughts and her work. She barely noticed her friends sitting next to her when they asked for her comments as they chattered away. She just nodded absently or laughed along with them. The pile of sorted tobacco grew larger and larger, so that several times she had to carry huge armfuls away to make room for more.

"Phorn! You can take the sorted tobacco to be weighed with the checker now. The village is a long way away, so we have to hurry up. You still have to pick up your younger brother, do the housework, fetch water, and make supper, don't you?"

Amphorn obediently did as she was told. Suddenly the full implication of her friend's reminder to hurry up dawned on her. What would happen if she went away to study? Then her mother would have to do all the housework alone. Mother was gaunt and fatigued from her work carrying cement. Her father had never let Amphorn do anything except her homework and reading. Her father was forever boasting to any and everyone that Amphorn was a clever student; but whenever the subject of Amphorn continuing her studies had arisen, her father's tone of voice would become bitter and he would try to change the subject.

Then Amphorn's mood lifted and she felt exuberant with the joy of her new decision. "I won't study! I won't study! Father, Mother, I'll stay at home and help you with your work, and I will work as well. Today I sorted eighty kilos of tobacco and got sixteen baht. Tomorrow I'll try to make at least twenty baht or maybe even more, like my friends. I'll get better and better at it. My small hands won't be worthless. They won't be worthless like they were studying in school. I won't be like *Phii* Kaew, the *kamnan's* daughter."

The sweat that had been running off her body evaporated quickly once in contact with the air outside the tobacco factory. Amphorn felt cool, cooler than ever before.

Khunthong's Tomorrow

The click-clack of the knitting machines reverberated in all directions, virtually drowning out the unceasing din of the cars and motorcycles passing on the street outside.

Khunthong carefully threaded the light-yellow wool into place with her left hand and with her right slid the machine handle back and forth. Knitting the wool into sweaters took time and effort, each movement adding only a strand's width. Some days Khunthong had to begin at 5 a.m. and work straight through until 10 p.m. On such days Khunthong could knit as many as ten long–sleeved sweaters; but she didn't like to work so fast, because afterwards she would ache from the tips of her fingers, her arms, her shoulders, all the way down to the small of her back. Normally Khunthong would knit only five or six sweaters a day.

In addition to carrying out her routine knitting of woolen sweaters for the cold season, Khunthong also had the added responsibility of teaching a new girl named Saenglaa. Saenglaa was about fourteen years old and acted as if she had never worked in her life. That was probably because she was the youngest child and used to doing as she pleased; her parents had sent her away to break her old habits and train her to work.

Khunthong was exasperated trying to teach Saenglaa. Her instructions and reminders, even though repeated over and over, seemed to get nowhere.

"Even though knitting may seem hard, it's still only indoor work. It's more comfortable than collecting clams or crabs, or digging for crickets and dung beetles, or gathering fruits and vegetables. Before one has found enough to eat, for just one meal, the sun has burnt one's skin black.

"Because you are a girl, if you want to go anywhere, you should tell me first. Not that you are confined here. But on days when there is a lot of work to be done, you shouldn't go anywhere.

"Living here you don't have to worry about getting rice or finding fish to eat. Even if the food isn't the best, it's not that different from what we eat at home in the village. And at the end of one year, they pay us 1,500 baht. Have you ever had that amount of money of your own in your life? Or your parents?

"After staying here with them a full year, you can hope to open a store and knit sweaters for a living. You won't need to be dependent on your parents anymore. You'll have a special skill. Here, they're paying four baht to have a sweater knit. If you're not knitting in bulk, but for individuals instead, you can charge a bit more."

Saenglaa always listened intently to her words, as if truly concentrating. Even though Saenglaa came from a village near the factory, Khunthong had no way of knowing that Saenglaa had never done any work, not even as little as having helped her parents catch a single fish. Saenglaa acted as if she didn't understand anything Khunthong was trying to teach her. She liked to move from one knitting machine to another and chatter away with the girls sitting next to her. In one day Saenglaa would only finish one or two sweaters.

"If I work hard, the owner will get that much richer. It's not fair. She gives us tidbits, but takes all she can. She thinks only of making money and doesn't care about anyone else. So why should we try to help her?"

The other girls laughed when they listened to Saenglaa talk like this. Some days Saenglaa did very peculiar things, like giving away any sweaters she had knit above her usual two to whichever girl had knit less than usual.

"Otherwise the factory owner will know that I've become good at knitting. If one day I'm feeling lazy and knit less than today, then she'll yell at me."

Early one morning, without anyone having even the slightest suspicion, Saenglaa gathered up her clothes and put them into a brown paper bag. Then, acting as if nothing unusual were happening and without saying goodbye to anyone, she walked out of the factory. Someone caught a fleeting glimpse of her back as she rounded the corner, but didn't dare tell anyone. She was afraid that the factory owner or her underlings might harm Saenglaa, as they had others before her.

As soon as the owner learned of Saenglaa's escape, she quivered with rage. She shouted for her husband and the two of them rushed down the stairs to the car. They drove to Saenglaa's house and returned just before noon, clearly in a foul mood.

"Has anyone seen my wall clock? It's missing. I'm sure Saenglaa took it. I'm going to report it to the police and have her arrested. You all will be witnesses for me."

"*Maenai*, Saenglaa didn't steal the clock. She didn't take anything with her that wasn't hers. The clock was huge. If Saenglaa had taken it, we would certainly have seen it. We saw Saenglaa leaving, and all she had with her was a single brown paper bag ."

"*Ee* Khunthong, there's no need for you to act as if you know everything. For all you know, she may have hidden it first. I say *Ee* Saenglaa stole it, and you will say whatever I tell you to say. Any trouble and I'll beat you until your eyes drop out. If anyone asks any of you, you are all to say *Ee* Saenglaa was the one who stole my clock. Understood?"

Maenai, heaving with fury, stomped down the stairs. A few moments later, the girls heard the sound of the car driving away from the factory, and they all sighed in relief.

"*Phii* Thong, just a little while ago I saw their son come and take the clock down himself. It wasn't Saenglaa who took it, for sure. But I was afraid to contradict *Maenai.*"

"I saw the same thing, *Phii* Thong. She's just trying to get Saenglaa into trouble. I feel so sorry for Saenglaa."

All anyone could talk about that afternoon was Saenglaa. They tried to guess Saenglaa's reasons for running away. Was it because the food was so terrible? Was it because they had to sleep on the floor in the same room where they worked, next to their machines? Was it because doing both the factory work and taking shifts doing *Maenai's* housework was too much for her? They recounted all the strange things Saenglaa had said, analyzing each in detail. Almost no knitting was done, lest the sound of the machines interfere with their discussion, which totally absorbed them until the factory owner returned.

"What's going on here? Have you girls decided to go on strike or what? Oh, you thankless wretches! Wings not yet brave, legs not yet strong, and already ungrateful. What do you have to say for yourselves? Hmm, *Ee* Khunthong, *Ee* Dyan, *Ee* Khiew, *Ee* Bun? You are clearly the ringleaders of this. Watch out or I will send the whole lot of you home. And I will fine you according to the contract, 200 baht a month. Think whether you will be able to pay me that or not. If you can't, I'll have you put in jail to teach you a lesson, you lot of good–for–nothings."

Khunthong felt her whole body getting hot. Her hands trembled and warm tears welled up and rolled down her cheeks. When she lifted her eyes and saw the angry expression on the owner's face, she was even more shocked. It took a moment to compose herself and find the strength to answer. "No, *Maenai.* We are not on strike or anything like that. But we don't feel right about some things and so we can't get back to work. We feel sorry for Saenglaa and are worried about her."

"Oh, so you are in with that good–for–nothing wretch, are you? You know she not only broke her contract with me, but also stole my wall clock. Do you remember your contract? Before any of you came to stay with me, you signed a contract. Do you remember what it said? Ee Khunthong and the rest of you have been with me for only eight months. Another four months until the year is up. So you'll be fined 800 baht each, isn't that right? Eight hundred baht, isn't it? And you won't get the 1,500 baht because you didn't stay the full year agreed to in the contract. So what is it? I'm interested to see just how foolhardy the lot of you are. Types like you, do you have the money? Eight hundred baht, you know."

Khunthong remained silent for a long time. She thought of Saenglaa's words. Saenglaa was right. *Maenai* thought only of money, how to spend as little as possible and get as much as she could. *Maenai* had no love lost for anyone; she had no sympathy for anyone. When she finally spoke, Khunthong's voice faltered, trembling with hurt and anger, "If that's the way you want to view things, fine. But, all of us were fond of Saenglaa and are worried about her. We don't want to be witnesses for you, because what you accuse her of just isn't the truth."

"You worthless beast! You ungrateful little upstart! Alright, tonight you go and find your own dinner. I'm not providing the likes of you with food or money. And I'm not letting you use my kitchen. If you want to go home and get fined, go ahead. If none of you have come to your senses by tomorrow, I'll send the lot of you home. And I'll enforce the terms of the contract as well."

With that, the factory owner stomped away. The girls sat in stunned silence, unable to fully grasp what had just happened. After a long time, they began whispering to each other, and slowly their voices grew louder and louder until they were speaking in normal tones.

"I'd like to go home, but I don't have the money for the fine, let alone the bus fare."

"Can I borrow one or two baht? I'd like to go and buy something to eat for tonight. Who's going to the market tonight? I'd like to buy one baht worth of sticky rice and fifty *satang* of fish sauce."

"Why don't we all go to the market together? Let's take advantage of the chance to get out for a change."

All the local boys in the vicinity gathered around, pleased to have the opportunity to admire these girls who so rarely came out of the factory building. But their enthusiastic cat calls, teasing, and outright pesterings came to no avail. None of the girls paid the slightest attention.

"Saenglaa!" Khunthong cried out with so much excitement she was almost shouting. Everyone in the marketplace turned to stare at her.

"*Phii* Thong!" Saenglaa stood up from where she had been sitting next to a set of small market baskets. The girls from the factory swarmed about her, all crying out at once. Saenglaa began to speak intently.

"*Maenai* followed me all the way to my home, but my father had already gone to see a lawyer. The lawyer said that the agreement we signed violated the labor laws. She can't fine us. But we can claim back wages from her. According to the law, we should have been getting paid no less than sixteen baht a day. If the employer pays for room and board and provides the knitting machines, then we get less, but we still should be earning something. Like me, I stayed one month, so I should have been paid at least 125 baht. And you don't have to worry about her saying that I stole her clock. She has no witnesses and no evidence. So none of you need be worried about me, but I am worried about all of you."

Saenglaa's words made everyone think. After dinner, when they had returned to the factory, no one wanted to work. Instead, they formed into a group and discussed the day's events intently.

"I want to go home like Saenglaa."

"Tonight we only spent one or two baht each on food, but we ate better than when *Maenai* feeds us."

"No wonder. *Maenai* gives us only thirty baht to go to the market to buy food for fifty of us. That's not even one baht per person."

"In the contract she said we came to study and practice knitting. That she would pay all our expenses. At the end of the year, she would pay us an additional 1,500 baht. But if anyone left before that, she would fine us 200 baht per month. I've been here for eight months, so I would be fined for four months or 800 baht."

"It's not fair. At first I thought using the knitting machines would be difficult. I thought it took years and years to learn. But in fact it only takes two or three weeks," another girl added.

"Actually, it might be difficult, if we were really taught something. But she only has us learn the two or three simple patterns that she wants to sell. She's just using us. If we wanted to knit some different designs that we liked, we'd have to figure out how to do them ourselves."

"If we came just to study, we would need to be here at most a month. But if we left after that month, we would have to pay a fine of 2,200 baht."

"But if we didn't leave and stayed on working, like Saenglaa said, we should be getting paid at least sixteen baht a day. What we pay her to study ends up more than the cost of our labor."

"Exactly. And we should be getting paid more than just sixteen baht a day because we don't just work during the day, but at night as well. Sometimes we hardly get any sleep at all."

"She really takes advantage of us. And on top of that, she's always yelling and insulting us as if we were less than human beings. Why should we have to endure all this for her?"

"Absolutely! Why should we have to endure all this?" many voices chimed in.

"If my home were close like Saenglaa's, I'd run away, too. But the bus fare back to the northeast is so expensive, nearly 200 baht," one girl said, her eyes watching Khunthong, who had appeared to be so close to the factory owner. The other girls fell silent and turned to watch Khunthong, waiting for her to speak.

Khunthong spoke slowly, but deliberately, "I would also like to run away, but we'll only get ourselves into trouble. She'll try to find some way to get us, for sure, like she tried to do to Saenglaa. Only our parents won't be able to get a lawyer to help us. Lawyers are said to be even more expensive than doctors."

"So you think we should just keep on with everything as it is now?"

"No, but we shouldn't go back without having enough for bus fare. If the law helps us, we should get our just wages, which we can use for bus fare to go home. We should force her to obey the laws."

"How?"

"If she doesn't obey the law, we'll refuse to work."

"If she does or she doesn't follow the law, it doesn't matter. We still won't work for her. I've had enough. I'm sick of it!"

"She's going to kick us out now and not give us a thing."

"That's right. The only way to force her is to make her kick us out and we refuse to leave until she pays us our wages."

"How will we feed ourselves?"

"That's not hard. We don't spend more than a few baht each day for food. Now some of us should write letters home and ask our families to help us. Whoever has money now should contribute it to the common fund. Then we should try to get our own supply of yarn and knit it ourselves or hire out knitting for other people. This time of year, there are lots of people who want knitting done. I'll help to find them," Khunthong concluded.

"What if she gets the police to evict us?"

"How can they evict us? We haven't done anything against the law. She's the one who broke the laws. If she wants to do something to us, there are fifty of us, so why should we be afraid? Isn't that right, *Phii* Thong?" another one said.

"Well, these are her house and her knitting machines."

"But part of what she owns has resulted from our labor."

"True. If she wants to kick us out, let her pay us our wages first, and we will have enough for bus fare home."

"O.K., so who wants to go home in this way?"

Everyone raised their hands. The chorus of voices became deafening.

"O.K., we'll start tomorrow," one person shouted.

Khunthong thought of the future she had been painting, of how she would be the first person in her village able to knit sweaters. But as she thought it over again, she didn't feel happy or sad anymore. After all, how many people in her village or even the whole district of Nong Bua Daeng had enough money to hire Khunthong to knit sweaters for them? Every year during the cold season, she had seen villagers sitting up close to small fires or wearing the blankets that the government had distributed. And where was Khunthong going to get the money to buy a knitting machine? If she still wanted to be a knitter of sweaters, she would no doubt have to remain a slave of the factory owner until the day she died.

"Alright. Tomorrow we'll be free."

Rit's First Mistake

It was of absolutely no concern to village youths like Rit whether there were droughts or floods destroying the rice in the fields. Rit didn't own any land; nor did his parents own any land. Furthermore, villagers who knew Rit were not the least bit willing to hire Rit or ask him to help them work their fields.* That was probably because they all despised and feared his laziness and unreliability. So, Rit didn't care if he farmed or if anyone else was able to farm or not. It didn't affect him in the least.

In Rit's village, if you didn't farm or hire yourself out as a field laborer, there was virtually no other way to make a living. Occasionally, the wealthier families in the village hired help, but there was no way Rit was going to hire himself out washing clothes or doing other household chores like his mother. Vigorous youths like him learned quickly that work of this kind was woman's work.

Similarly, it would be hard for Rit to catch fish or gather plants that grew wild in public places. Rit felt that should be the job of old people, not youths like himself. He had never seen any of his friends do such work. In fact, he had never seen any of his friends do any work at all, not even the ones who had studied in school and graduated. But they still had better clothes. They always had cigarettes to smoke and money to spend. Some of them even had motorcycles to ride. This was because they got the money from their parents.

Rit was resentful towards his mother and father. He felt sorry that he had been born into a poor family and into a poor lineage. Rit had tried to find out about his family background. He learned that every one of his relatives was poor, and they had been poor for as many generations as anyone could remember. His mother hired herself out to do whatever work was available, from washing clothes and drawing well water to cleaning floors.

---

*There are three main labor patterns used in northern Thailand. One is wage labor, where the worker is paid in cash. The second is exchange labor, where villagers work on each other's fields. The third is euphemistically called "helping," but is, in fact, a form of hired labor in which the worker is paid in kind, usually in bushels of rice at harvest time. The worker must wait to be paid until harvest, but has the advantage that he is then generally paid more.

His father had gone off and taken a minor wife in a different sub-district. That was after he had gotten out of jail for a theft charge. But his mother had never been bitter that his father had left her. She had explained to Rit that it had been necessary for him to steal and necessary for him to go and live elsewhere. People in this village hadn't liked his father. His being an ex–convict had been all the more reason for everyone here to look down on him and despise him.

Rit had thought of becoming a thief like his father, but his mother was forever saying he wouldn't make much of a thief, just as his father hadn't either. But whenever anything disappeared in the village, villagers would question Rit suspiciously, even though he hadn't stolen it. They just assumed he was like his father. Rit defended his name by watching to make sure his friends didn't steal anything from anyone in their village.

Rit had never been all that upset though about the standard of living of his family. His friends often helped him out with food and other things. They were glad to help him since Rit was a good friend to have. Rit cared for his friends and stood by them, even to the death if necessary. By the same token, if someone was Rit's enemy or displeased him, he did so at his own peril.

Rit wanted to be a gunman or a thief because these were the only jobs in the region he could do. But so far, he had not met with the proper opportunity for these kinds of jobs. He only wanted to kill or rob rich people; but so far, if he were really to engage in these activities, he would have had to do so at the expense of other poor people. Only rich people had the money to hire gunmen to kill others, even though the going rate was 500 baht. As far as he could tell, only poor people got shot and killed for free. And only poor people got robbed. They had no way of buying a gun to protect their property and no way to pay the costs involved in pressing charges.

It was no great surprise when Rit got a job working for a politician running for office during the last election.[*] Rit did an outstanding job. He was able to ensure that no one tore down his candidate's campaign posters, At the same time, he succeeded in tearing down the campaign posters of many competing candidates and, in general, disrupting their campaigning. In addition, he did so well in his security detail that the candidate grew very fond of Rit. He often took Rit with him on trips into town. Once Rit opened his mouth to say that he wanted to find work in town, the candidate promised to help get him a job.

*   *   *

"Oh no, sir. I wouldn't have one of your boys simply be an usher. There's no future in that—they just stay ushers all their lives. I'll have him practice up

---

*This is a reference to the violent elections of April 1976.

in the projection room. That's much better. It opens up many more possibilities. And if there's another election, he can help you show the films. They're always the best way to gather a good crowd. It'll make vote–getting that much easier for you."

Rit was so happy he almost danced when he heard the manager talk like this. He would now be able to watch every film being shown in that movie theatre. He'd be able to see films more often than any of his friends in the village.

The manager looked Rit over from head to feet. Then he pressed a buzzer to summon a woman who entered the room.

"Would you please take this boy to meet Lek? Tell Lek that he should arrange quarters for him and teach him how to work the projection equipment. He'll have an assistant now."

Rit was sorry to have to leave the beautiful room, comfortably cooled by a machine, with pleasant songs piped in to listen to all the time. After taking his departure from the candidate and thanking the manager, Rit went off, following the girl as told.

He met Lek in a cramped, dark and stuffy room, bordering on overwhelmingly humid. It was packed with all kinds of equipment. Lek had a slight build, was about thirty years old, and had Chinese-style eyes.[*] He was busy working. After they finished introducing themselves, Lek began explaining some of the things in the room to Rit.

"It's just about time for the noon show. Have you had lunch yet? If not, hurry up and eat. After the noon show, there's another one at two in the afternoon."

"I don't have to eat yet. I can wait until after the showings. I really want to learn how to do this as soon as I can."

Rit toyed lovingly with the movie projector until Lek felt irritation, as well as empathy.

"You'll get paid five baht per show. On weekdays there are four shows and on weekends there are six shows. The lodging is free here, but we have to pay for meals. Sometimes we also have to do other odd jobs."

Rit nodded his head. He let his mind wander so that he barely heard all the explanations that Lek was giving.

"If we both help each other, we can save one of the projectors. Just the cost of one projector bulb easily pays your wages."

Rit hadn't understood what Lek said, but Lek didn't pay any attention. Lek kept on talking as if he wanted to go on forever.

---

[*]Unlike the population of rural areas, urban populations are overwhelmingly Chinese in origin. This difference in historical and racial origin is often apparent in the differences in the shape of the eyes.

"It's kind of hot in here. It gets even hotter when the projector is running. I once asked them to make a hole so the air-conditioning could come through, but they wouldn't. They were afraid the noise of the projector would be heard and would bother the movie-goers."

Rit didn't understand this either, as he didn't know what air-conditioning was, and if the room was hot, there was a fan. This was already too good to be true.

"Wow, it's almost time to start the movie. Come and look at this first."

Rit rushed over eagerly.

"These are called slides. They look easy, even though they're not very interesting or fun to watch. But they are very hard to use. If you don't do it right, you'll get a lot of complaints. They may cut your pay or even fire you. They belong to businessmen who hire us to show them to advertise their merchandise. Most of them are good friends of the manager here. If you make the slightest mistake, they go straight to the manager to complain. We have to be very careful. Make sure you don't get them in upside down or backwards. When you pick them up, you have to hold them like this, with your fingers like this. This is how you put them in. This is how you take them out. Watch me first."

Lek started teaching him the first lesson. Rit concentrated so hard he felt tired from all the excitement. But before the slides were finished, Rit was bored and anxious for them to end. He wanted to learn how to use the movie projector. They were really no fun, just like Lek said. The audience probably didn't want to watch them either. He didn't know what right the businessmen had to force everyone to watch them. It wasn't as if this were a free showing like the medicine shows in the villages.*

"The hard part of projecting movies is winding and unwinding the film, and when the one reel is finished and you have to switch machines. You have to time it just right. You can't let the film jerk or skip. This machine is all ready to go. If you want to turn the machine on, you push this switch here. After you have let the reel wind to the right point, you push this switch to start the movie."

Lek patiently taught Rit everything, bit by bit, until Rit was eventually able to do showing after showing by himself. At first, Rit thought it was fun; but as time went on, it became sheer torment. Rit had to watch each film tens of times over, and nearly all were rehashes of the same plot, especially the Thai

---

*Even today there are people who travel from village to village selling medicine. They show free movies to collect a crowd and advertise their products before, in between, and after reels. This custom is slowly becoming less common in villages near big cities, where people have direct access to television and movie theaters.

and Chinese films. Every day, the two of them had to endure the stuffiness, sitting in the cramped, dark, hot room. On top of that, they were always having to work. If it were a weekday, he had to be in the projection booth from before noon until five, when they had a break to shower and eat. Then they had to go back at seven and stay until nearly midnight. The rest of their time that was more or less free was taken up with petty chores like cleaning up their sleeping quarters, which they took turns doing. There were also odd jobs like putting up posters, carrying films, cleaning the projectors, or previewing new films, depending on what had to be done. On weekends and holidays, when there were two additional showings, there was no free time to catch a breath at all.

Rit and Lek sometimes took turns being alone in the projection booth during the times that one of them wanted to take a rest or go off and have some fun at a local festival. But they didn't do that very often, because it was very tiring being alone in the booth. There was always the risk of falling asleep while watching the projector. So the two of them helped each other, show after show. But this day, Lek needed to rest. If he didn't, he would get even sicker than he was already.

Rit had not seen the manager since he had begun working there almost a month ago. He was shocked to see the manager yanking the door open and storming into the projection room. His face was scowling, his voice shrill as he asked, "Where's Lek?"

"He's not feeling well, sir. He's sleeping in the room downstairs," Rit answered, his voice quivering.

"What kind of job are you doing projecting? Why haven't you adjusted the focus?"

"What's the focus, sir?" Rit honestly had never heard this word before.

"What! Lek didn't teach you? Everyone in the audience has been complaining, ever since the first show. You idiot! What kind of a job do you think you're doing? Almost a month and you still don't know anything. All you know is how to eat and pick up your pay. Get out! And tell Lek he can look for another job as well. I don't want either of you around here anymore. Go! Get out of here now! I'll project myself. Get out of my sight!"

Rit was speechless. No sooner had Rit passed through the door of the projection booth than the manager slammed it shut.

" *Phii* Lek, the manager has fired both of us. He said I hadn't fixed the focus when I was showing the movie."

Lek was starting to feel better. He got up in amazement.

"Huh? What? My god, it's true! I didn't teaching you about that. We were always doing it together. Usually it doesn't have to be adjusted; it doesn't change much. You must have been using the third projector. The lens on that projector isn't very good. You must not have been watching, or the film must not have been any good."

"Brother, I watched it until I was bored stiff, I don't know how many shows. I was busy rewinding the other reel."

"Well, if we're fired, we're fired. It's my mistake; it's not your fault. Don't feel bad. In a city like this, there's lots of work. Someone as strong as you can easily find work in construction. The pay is better, too. I'll take you to apply for work myself."

Rit was quite happy to be able to work construction. From the day he'd been born, he'd never built anything from bricks and cement. He was curious to see how they did it.

"Good luck, Rit. You'll get paid twenty-two baht a day. If you are a carpenter or bricklayer, you can earn fifty to sixty baht a day. Too bad you've only had experience handling bamboo.* Try this and see what happens. Who knows, you may be able to become a carpenter or bricklayer yet. Oh, but one important point. You have to be careful. Your boss is widely known. If you do anything to upset him, there is no way you'll ever get another job in construction. Don't forget that. I'm going to take off. Visit me when you have free time. I'm going to try to get a job projecting for the medicine shows."

Rit liked construction work much better than showing films. He was happy exercising his body. He was glad to be outside in the open air. He enjoyed teasing and joking with fellow workers, both male and female. He didn't have to endure the loneliness of sitting in the projection room with no one to talk to but Lek.

Most of his fellow workers lived in villages near town, so it wasn't necessary for them to sleep in town like him. That's why Rit was able to get a comfortable room of his own at the construction site. It was also the reason why Rit was able to develop closer, more intimate ties with the boss than any of the other workers.

One night the contractor stopped by and talked with the night watchmen.

"Well, Rit, those damn building inspectors are hassling me. They're saying that for the four or five foundation posts at the south end, the cement wasn't mixed right, that we'll have to tear them down. I told you all to hurry up and coat the cement, but you didn't listen to me. At this rate, I'm going to lose money for sure. Tomorrow I'll probably stop by in the afternoon. I'm going to see if there is any other way first. So don't have anyone do anything with those posts just yet. I'll come and tell you if we're going to tear them down or not."

The next afternoon, some of the workers were assigned to tear down the faulty posts and supports. The sound of hammers pounding concrete rang out ceaselessly. White dust floated everywhere, clouding out the sun so that all that was left of it was a faint glow. As soon as the first post came crashing down,

---

*Poor people's houses in the villages are generally made from bamboo. Only wealthier villagers have homes of wood or brick. Scaffolding on construction sites is often made from bamboo.

startled yells could be heard everywhere. Lots of people ran over to the site, shouting and hollering in such confusion that it was impossible to make out their words. Then one worker ran out, screaming at the top of his voice, "Hey! You've got to help Met! Help Met!"

Many hands and many muscles helped to lift the post. The iron rods that were sticking out were still attached to the base. Met's body lay stretched out on his back. His hands were rigid and twitching in spasms. His eyes were rolled back. Blood streamed from his mouth and nose. His indigo blue village shirt*was coated chalky white where the post had come crashing down against his chest, turning dark red with the flow of blood.

"Let's get him to the hospital." Rit was the first to rush in. He embraced Met's body and pulled it out from under the post that many people were straining to hold up. As soon as Rit had dragged Met's body free, the post was released and fell back to the ground. It made a terrifying thud as it landed. Lots of people rushed to help Rit carry the body.

"Let's go to the hospital. There's a hospital close to here. Hurry, hurry, hurry! Met can't die!"

*   *   *

"Doctor, doctor, you've got to help Met. A concrete post just fell on him."

"Lay him down on the stretcher first. Hospital regulations require that every patient pay a deposit of 500 baht first."

"Boss, the doctors are asking for 500 baht first. Boss, please give them the deposit."†

"Rit, I don't have any money right now. I've just taken the building inspectors to lunch. Why don't we take him to another hospital? You can put him in my car. But I don't think it's really necessary. Met is beyond help. Just look; his chest is all caved in."

"But he's still breathing. He's not dead yet. Doctor, please help him! Boss, please! Met, don't die on us yet. Please, doctor, please help him. The government hospital is too far away. Please doctor. Boss ..." Rit pleaded.

Met lay there on the hospital stretcher. His breath was shallow. His spasms had subsided somewhat. Everyone was watching in utter silence. Blood still oozed. Met's lips quivered.

"In just a few more minutes he'll be dead," someone behind Rit murmured.

---

*Villagers are characteristically dressed in cotton dark-blue indigo shirts and pants.

†Unlike government hospitals, private hospitals often require payment before giving treatment. Although Met is calling the hospital staff "doctors," they may well have been admission clerks.

"His family should get some kind of compensation pay," another voice spoke up. Rit's ears perked up but his eyes didn't move from his injured friend.

"But how much will they get? He wasn't a permanent worker."

"Depends on what they do. If just the contractor pays, they'll only get a few thousand. But if they have the Labor Department arrange matters, they'll probably get twenty or thirty thousand baht."

"So then why don't they notify the Labor Department?"

"Villagers don't know about it."

"So why doesn't anyone tell them?"

"Who would dare?"

Rit was just turning his head to look at the person talking, when some one cried out, "Met just died."

Rit felt he would faint. All the workers stood motionless. Tears welled in their eyes. Some of the girls began sobbing and sobbing. Three or four police-men got out of their car.

"Alright, everyone, please go back to work. Those of you who actually saw the accident, tell the police what happened."

The workers started to gather, but no one wanted to leave.

"I will help pay for the funeral. I'll pay his mother and father 3,000 baht," the contractor announced proudly.

"In that case, his parents should go to the Labor Department. Then they'd get more than that." Rit spoke without meaning to say anything to upset the contractor. He didn't have the slightest idea where the Labor Department would get the money to pay.

"Rit, what are you saying? You can get right back to work, right now." The contractor's face was red, but he controlled his temper to speak in a normal tone.

Rit started to open his mouth, but the contractor rushed over and grabbed Rit by his shirt collar. He was shaking Rit, shrieking out of control, "If you open your mouth again, I'll hit you!"

But it was too late. No sooner had the contractor raised his fist in what was just a threat, than Rit's well-developed instinct to fight took over. His fist shot out, full force. The contractor reeled and fell. Rit had stepped back ready for the next blow when the police put a stranglehold on him from the back.

"Getting fired this time was my mistake," Rit murmured quietly to himself.

Before Dawn

The late afternoon sky was black. The tips of the bamboo swayed madly under the violent wind. Leaves from trees of every description blew in the air. Dust rose up in clouds. Thunder crashed across the sky. And then the rains poured down. Chill rain gusted past the eaves. Sao, a middle–aged man, sat shivering in the cold.

"Long, Long, could you bring me the plastic sheet? It's really raining hard. Any minute now, it'll be leaking through onto the mattresses." Fighting the pounding rain, he shouted to his wife who was busily lining up buckets behind the house.

"Wait a second! I'm wearing it. I want to get these buckets ready. This way we can collect some rainwater. It's really pouring heavily. It's already leaking into the kitchen," his wife yelled back.

"We're already soaked to the skin," his children, who were making supper, shouted.

"Bear with it just a bit longer," he yelled back, without thinking.

His house was like that of other poor people in the village, made entirely of bamboo with a thatch roof. There was just one room in the house and the rest consisted essentially of a porch surrounded by a bamboo wall the height of someone sitting down. Rain easily blew past the gap between the wall and the roof, and on day like this, when it rained heavily, there was virtually no spot in the house except the sleeping room where they could hope to keep dry.

This day was even worse than usual. The rain had come earlier than most years, before they had had a chance to change the thatch. This year they'd have to change nearly the entire roof, since they had simply been replacing and repairing the old thatch a bit at a time for the past three or four years now. But so far they hadn't even gathered half the thatch they would need. Thatch was hard to find this year, and they would have to buy the rest from other villages. But at the moment, they still didn't have enough money. So it wasn't his fault that the other members of the family would have to endure the torments of that day.

He was startled from his reverie when his wife yelled out in surprise, "*Phii*, *Phii* Sao! Some stranger is sitting under our house! *Phii*, find out who it is."

"Look, Father. Right under where you're sitting."

He looked between the slats in the bamboo floor. Lightning flashed, illuminating for an instant the shape of a man sitting huddled up, shivering with the cold, beneath him.

"Who are you? What are you doing under the house?" he called down, somewhat shocked.

"No one, only me. I'd just like to rest here, out of the rain, for a little while."

"Where are you from?" he shouted down, trying to be heard over the rain.

"From town. I was on my way home, but then it started to rain so hard."

"Well, why don't you come on up inside the house. It's freezing cold down below. The rain will drain all your strength away."

The stranger got up and climbed up the ladder into the house. His white baggy shirt and pants were soaking wet and covered with mud. He was strongly built. He gave a fleeting smile and sat down near the ladder.

Sao was about to begin a conversation with the man, but his wife came, bringing the plastic sheet with her. So he silently took the sheet and went into the sleeping room.

"*Phiichaaj*, where do you come from? How did you get here?" his wife asked.

"I came from town. I was on my way home, but then it started raining so hard that I couldn't keep going." His voice was even, his answer not differing much from what he had said while under the house.

"So how did you get this far? Did you walk all the way from town?" Long asked again.

"No, not quite. I had three baht on me to pay the bus fare. They made me get off at the entrance to Baan Du village, so I had to walk the rest of the way myself. The fare to my home is twelve baht. I only had three baht, so the bus wouldn't take me all the way." He smiled self-consciously.

Saw stepped out of the sleeping room, carrying in his hand a *phaakhaomaa*,* and sat down next to the man.

"Why don't you change out of your clothes. They're soaking wet. What you're wearing looks like a hospital uniform. Did you just come from hospital?"

"Yes, I've just come from hospital."

---

*A *phaakhaomaa* is a piece of multi-purpose woven cloth used by village males. It may be tied around their heads as a turban, loosely thrown over one shoulder as a kind of handkerchief or facecloth, tied around the waist as a belt, worn as an informal loincloth, or used in many other ways.

"Are you ill? You look strong and healthy."

"They say I'm crazy. I've just come from the mental hospital." He spoke firmly and clearly, his voice ringing out as if he wanted everyone in the world to know.

The husband and wife gasped in surprise. The two turned to look at each other, the *phaakhaomaa* frozen in Sao's hands. Both children in the kitchen grabbed hold of knives.

"Oh, there's no need to be afraid of me. I'm not that crazy. It's just that there are some times when I don't know what I'm doing. But I've never harmed anyone. I'm in full control of myself now."

"*Phiichaaj*, why were you in such a rush to leave? Why didn't you stay until you were properly recovered?" Long asked apprehensively.

Tears rolled down the man's face, mixing with the drops of rain that already streaked his face. He reached for the *phaakhaomaa* in Sao's hand to wipe away the tears from his eyes. Long turned to admonish her children, who were staring at the man entranced.

"Hurry up and get some food ready, children. And as soon as it's ready, bring it in."

"If I'd stayed there, I would have gotten even crazier instead of better. I was there for a long time and no one paid any attention to me. Even my relatives and family stopped visiting me. Once in an eternity my wife would come. I hardly ever got to see my children. The bus fare from home to the hospital is expensive, there and back about twenty-four baht per person. It wasn't as if they had nothing else to do. The money she earned in a day she needed to feed the family with. Just earning five to ten baht a day is already difficult."

"But surely the doctors took good care of you, didn't they?"

The man shook his head dejectedly. "They're good, but they're over–burdened with work. There are 6–700 patients, but fewer than ten doctors. I didn't know what to do. Some months I never got to talk with the doctor at all. But even more, I missed my home, my wife, and my children. If I'm going to die, I want to be allowed to die at home."

"Where do you live?" Sao asked as he lit the kerosene lamp to chase away the darkness.

"Thaen Khao Luang village."

"Oh no! That's still a long way from here. How can you hope to walk all that way?"

"It doesn't matter. I'll just keep walking and eventually I'll get there."

"We wish we could help you with the bus fare, but we don't have any money ourselves."

Although the wind had finally died down, the rain was still falling heavily. Over and over again rain dropped off the thatch onto the three underneath, but none of them made any effort to do anything about it. There were leaks nearly everywhere. The children had fled to the back of the house, but it was leaking there just as much.

"Are you afraid of walking around alone? You might get attacked by a *phi-idutlyat*."*

"A what? A *phiidutlyat*? I've never heard of them. But I'm not afraid of spirits or ghosts or such–like. I'm more afraid of my fellow man."

"But everyone is talking about them. That the *phiidutlyat* are on the rampage. They suck blood to give to the communists."

"I don't know anything about *phiidutlyat*, let alone communists."

"They say they all look the same. Most have long hair. And they usually carry shoulder bags and wear sandals."

"While I was living at the hospital in town, I saw lots of people like this coming to visit. I didn't see that they did anyone any harm. They said they were students. They often came to assist the doctors."

"Sounds like the same group all right," Long concluded briefly.

Sao had been watching the raindrops leaking down from the thatch roof, saying nothing. But now he spoke.

"A couple of days ago the radio broadcast that there were two or three people in this area who were attacked by *phiidutlyat* and since then have never been seen or heard from again. Until this day, not even their bodies have been found." He paused and cleared his throat before continuing, "Actually though, they didn't disappear. They ran off with friends to Bangkok ..."

Sao was interrupted by a noise in the back of the house where his children had been preparing supper.

"Mother, food is ready."

"So bring it in. *Phiichaaj*, please join us for supper," Long said.

"Bring the food over here. The rain leaks through least here," Sao said.

Several times during the evening gusts of wind blew up again, and each time the kerosene lamp flickered and nearly was blown out. Long had to cup her hand around the flame several times. The chill seeped through to their very bones.

---

*Phiidutlyat literally means a "ghost who sucks blood." Even though many Thai villagers still believe in *phii* (spirits of various kinds), no mention was ever made in traditional village folklore of *phiidutlyat*. Stories of *phiidutlyat* began circulating in 1975–1976 in an effort to counter students' activities in the rural areas and were given considerable publicity both in newspapers and over the radio. These rumored ghosts had many characteristics similar to university students and the Western Dracula, but were supposedly active both in the daytime and at night. They allegedly appeared in various places, some using cars to carry away their victims and bringing buckets to contain the blood. For more on the general context of this manipulation of village superstitions, see the Introduction.

"I haven't eaten food like this for such a long time. It makes me more homesick than ever for my family." The man ate vigorously.

Afterwards, the man, children, husband, and wife sat around talking, as if they were close relatives finally reunited after a long absence. At one point Long asked, "*Phii*, were you depressed or unhappy about something in particular so that you had to go to hospital?"

Tears welled up and rolled down his cheek. "I don't really like having to think about any of it. I still don't understand up to the present day what's the matter with me, that I have to end up like this."

The rains fell even harder. Lightning streaked across the sky and thunder growled and groaned. But the couple was oblivious to all except what the man had to say.

"Originally, I was an ordinary farmer. I had a small plot of land of my own, just enough to support my family comfortably for the rest of our lives. That was up until 1973, when the government decided to build an irrigation canal with a road on one side that passed through my land. All that was left was about half a meter on one side. Not enough to do anything with. I was totally destitute that year, supporting myself by working as hired labor on the irrigation canal construction. We earned enough to live on, on a day–to–day basis. I waited a year before I was finally reimbursed for the value of my land. I had over four *rai* of paddyfield—for which I received the real equivalent of just over one *rai*. The little bit of land that was left wasn't enough to do anything with. But they didn't compensate me for that—only for the land they actually surveyed for the irrigation canal. And they bought it for less than the price I had paid for the land over ten years ago."

He shifted his position and leaned back against one of the posts of the house, exhausted.

"I received just over 10,000 baht. After paying off debts and other expenses, all that was left was enough to buy only one single *rai* of land. I didn't know what to do. I decided to use the money as a down payment on a second–hand mini–truck from a car dealer in town. I transported goods and passengers all over the area and earned enough money to support my wife and children."

He lifted the *phaakhaomaa* to dry his eyes.

"I earned money to pay the monthly installments to the car dealer and supported my family for two years. I earned enough to make ends meet day by day. I had thought in another three months, when I would have finished the monthly payments, I'd be able to start living more comfortably."

His jaws tightened, and his eyes bulged frighteningly.

"But then one day, the owner of the company from which I bought the car was arrested by the police on charges of being the head of a car–stealing racket. At first I didn't believe that someone as rich as that could be a thief. After a few more days lots of other people who had bought cars from that company were also arrested by police on charges of having bought stolen property. I was the ninth person to be arrested."

Even though the sound of pouring rain and thunder hadn't stopped, everything was still, as if utter silence had fallen.

"I had already made two years' worth of payments on that car. I had passed police numerous times on my way back and forth. I had a driver's license. I paid the taxes each year. My car was inspected by the police each year. Why didn't the police say anything before? Why didn't they tell me earlier? They let me pay 50–60,000 baht, so that I had almost finished all the payments on the car. Why did they have to arrest me then?"

His voice was almost breaking, but then grew calmer after a deep breath.

"The owner of the company wasn't in jail for long—he was able to get off scot-free. It's normal that rich people who get arrested don't stay in jail for long. I was in jail for about one month until I was released. But that was because I was crazy and they had already confiscated everything I owned."

He stopped talking and once again used the *phaakhaomaa* to dry away his tears. The rain still hadn't let up. The floor of the house was drenched from all the rain that had leaked through the thatch. The listeners sat in silence for a long moment.

"I'm very sorry," Long tried to console him, but wasn't able to say any more than that.

Sao kept his gaze fixed on the bamboo floor, as if examining the patterns of the raindrops splashing up off the floor. Finally he turned to look at the face of the man. "I'm very sorry. Our house is full of leaks. Would you like to spend the night with us? On the other hand, if you stayed here, you probably wouldn't get much sleep unless the rain gives up. It's really leaking badly everywhere. How would it be if we took you over to *Lung* Kaew's house to sleep?"

"Never mind. I came to this village because I thought I might look up an old friend who lives at the far end of the village. I was thinking I might stay with him overnight. *Ai* Thaa, with the owl-eyes."

"Oh, so you know *Ai* Thaa, do you? Well, we can go over there later on then. Today he'll be home for sure. This afternoon I saw him riding his bicycle past back and forth several times."

"Actually, I might as well go over there now. It's getting late and I could use a good night's sleep."

"How can you think of going now!? It's still pouring rain and so dark out without the stars. You can't see a thing."

"But if I were to wait for the rain for stop, I'd be here a long time. It seems to have let up a bit now. Could I perhaps ask to borrow your plastic rainsheet and perhaps your flashlight? I'll return them to you tomorrow morning."

"I don't see why not. Of course you can. Long, would you go and get them for him?"

The man's manner seemed more calm and relaxed now than when he had first come into the house. He accepted the flashlight and rainsheet that they gave him and tried to cover himself as best he could. He smiled as he offered his thanks and left the house.

"See you tomorrow then. I'd like to escort you to the other end of the village, but we have only the one rainsheet."

After he had gone, Long said quietly to her husband, "I feel so sorry for him. Tomorrow morning I'll try to cook some really nice food for him. Seems tonight we and the children will probably all have to sleep in the same room together. I just took the plastic sheet you had fixed over the mosquito nets. It had already collected enough water to fill a wash basin. But if we put the mattresses right up to the door and sleep close together, we can probably avoid the leaks. It's a good thing that this room doesn't leak any more than this."

The thunder and lightening had subsided, but the rain was still falling gently. The sound of the various frogs could be heard from all around. Long blew out the lamp. Just as they were about to go to sleep and were half–asleep already, they heard the sounds of cheering and yelling in the distance. And the sounds of dogs howling and barking for a while. And then that too fell silent.

"A bunch of drunken clowns are having another fight, it seems," Sao grumbled.

After they had fallen asleep, a voice suddenly called out at the foot of the stairs to their house, "Sao, Sao, are you asleep yet?"

"No, not yet. Why? What is it, Kham?" Sao recognized the voice.

"Just a while ago did someone wearing a white shirt and white pants come here?"

"Yes, in fact he had supper with us. Why? What's the matter?" Sao got up quickly and went out of the room. Long was lighting the kerosene lamp.

"He's already dead. They beat him to death. I thought I recognized your flashlight and rainsheet, so I thought I would stop by and make sure."

"What happened? What went on?" both husband and wife cried, shocked.

"At first I heard the screams of a child who had gone to collect some mangoes that had blown off in the wind, yelling "*Phiidutlyat, phiidutlyat!*" Everyone living near my house went crazy. By the time I got dressed and went out to look, he was already dead, his face beaten beyond recognition. I was worried that he might already have sucked up your blood and made off with your rainsheet and flashlight as well.

"You should be careful, you know. The government is broadcasting over the radio every day to be on the watch for *phiidutlyat*. They suck blood to give to the communists. Oh, I've hidden your rainsheet and flashlight already. So don't worry. I was afraid others might recognize them as well and start accusing you of having joined hands with the communists.

"Our village headman will probably get some sort of prize for being the first in this area to kill a *phiidutlyat*. He was beaming and looking happy. Said if he really got the award, he would host a feast for the whole village.

"Hey, what's the matter with the two of you? You're not saying anything."

Kao Ying!

A group of small children were huddled together playing in a dirt compound near the *je chor*,* their shrieks of merriment such that none of them paid any attention to the sounds of barking dogs coming from the village gateway.

The children's gaze was focussed on the bare ground in front of them where two golden–yellow wasps, black stripes glistening around their abdomens, were clasped in battle. When the wasps separated, the small children used sticks to goad them back together again.

Normally the wasp is a frightening insect. Its savage instinct compels it to sting everything that comes into contact with it, even without intending to. The poison of just one sting is sufficient to stupefy a grown man and, if attacked by swarms, even elephants succumb. But now they had become the playthings of children who had nothing but broad leaves with which to swat them down if they tried to fly off and thin sticks to irritate them into fighting each other once they fell to the ground.

The barking of the dogs grew louder and more frequent. The children became temporarily quiet. At that moment, four or five well–built strangers appeared. At first it looked like they might stop to rest at the *je cho*r, but then changed their minds and walked on toward the children.

"*Mua loh khatyy,*" one of the top–knotted, grimy–faced children looked up and greeted the unknown men apprehensively. Not one of them answered the little boy. But the poorest dressed member of the group of strange men turned around and whispered to his companions, "He asked us where we are going, but don't pay any attention to him. He can't understand your language, *jaonai.*"

"*Kao Ying*! Victory!" another of the children yelled, and an excited chorus of indistinguishable chatter rose up. The children who had taken an interest in

---

*Rest sites in the clearings in the mountain forests near Hmong villages. The Hmong are one of the most populous of the hill tribes living in the mountains of northern Thailand. Hmong also live in the mountains of Laos, Vietnam, and southern China.

the strangers now turned to stare at one of the wasps that had died in battle. It was being poked and shoved back and forth by an exuberant child with a wooden stick.

"He said he won," the same stranger said vacantly as he walked away. A small black pig with a curving spine fled with its offspring to the side of the path.

"*Lao* Sii!" a villager who was walking along the path cried out excitedly.

"*Lao* Syy!" came the reply, no less excitedly.

"*Jaonai*, sir, this is *Lao* Syy. He is an old friend of mine. We have known each other since the days we both lived on Mae Chaem Mountain. We haven't seen each other for over ten years now."

The man addressed as *jaonai* smiled blandly in response, as he observed *Lao* Syy folding his hands and bowing Chinese-style while inviting them to visit his home.

"*Lao* Sii, so, how is it living in the lowlands?" the host asked as he passed cups of tea around.

"So–so. Trying to make a living is rough–going. Not like up here in the mountains."

"So, tell me about it. We listen to the radio broadcasts in our language. The radio says that our people living in the lowlands are doing well."

"It's not true. It's not true. Land is scarce and money is hard to come by. It doesn't compare with staying in the mountains and growing opium for sale. Here in the mountains, however much money one needs, one can get; however much land one needs, one can have. And when one has finished planting, it's easily sold and the prices are better."

"So, what have you come here for? Have you come back here to live?"

"No, I'm not coming back. I made my decision to leave. Before I left, my mother and father and brothers and sisters all forbade me, but I didn't listen. If I can't make good, I certainly won't come back. I would be ashamed before my friends."

"So you've just come visiting for fun?"

Lao Syy glanced over to the group of policemen. He saw them scrutinizing the various possessions in his house. *Lao* Sii edged over to sit a bit closer.

"My boss wants to get a hold of some goods to sell. You wouldn't happen to have any, would you?"

"No, we didn't plant any. But if you want some, we could probably find some for you. How many packages were you thinking of getting?"

"How heavy is one package?" the *jaonai* asked, speaking for the first time.

"One package is equivalent to a *joy*, or one kilo 600 grams."

"How much is a *joy*?"

"The going price around here runs 2,500 baht."

"We'd like, say, one hundred packages. Can you get that much?"

"Uh, that's difficult, sir. Around here the most you can hope to find anywhere is about nine or ten packages."

"Alright, then give us ten packages. When can it be ready?"

"What day would you like to have it, sir?"

"How about in three days time?

"Fine. Or if you wanted it today, that could be arranged."

"No, in three days is better. In three days if you could send it to the road at Mon Korm Mountain, we'll bring a pick–up truck and load it on there."

"What about coming and picking it up here?"

"The pickup couldn't make it up here. There's also a greater chance that someone might notice it. You bring it to us; that's the best way."

Lao Syy talked for a long time with *Lao* Sii in their native language. In the end they agreed. After a few more moments of exchanges, according to custom, the strange group of men bade farewell and left.

At dawn of the appointed day, *Lao* Syy felt a shiver of horror flash suddenly down his spine when he saw the signal from *Lao* Sii, his old friend—a cross mark that symbolized enemy carved in the branch of a tree.

Lao Syy felt confused. He didn't want trouble with anyone. But for him to acquire the ten *joy* of opium he was carrying, he had had to invest a lot of capital and labor, clearing the forest, digging the hard–packed earth, pulling out the weeds in an area of no less than ten rai. Even though it was fertile soil, the most he got from one rai of land was only one finished package of raw opium. Producing opium is far more difficult and back breaking than planting rice because it is done by human labor alone. There was no way he would let anyone cheat or steal him out of it.

Lao Syy quickly called his group together to talk over how to solve the problem. They decided to have *Lao* Taw and *Lao* Chong be the ones to make the actual delivery. *Lao* Syy and the rest of a group of over ten people would hide in wait in the jungle along the roadside, just in case. *Lao* Sang closed the discussion with the resolve that all present felt deeply:

"Even though they are government officials, police are also involved in the trade. If this gang thinks it can confiscate what is ours for nothing, they're not decent men, but outright bandits. If their aim was to arrest us, then why haven't they arrested others, in other places, as well? If they're really going to arrest *Lao* Syy, then why haven't they ever arrested *Lao* Sang? If it's going to be this way, then they're not good people. No need to let them live."

The goods were safely loaded on the pick–up truck, when suddenly the faces of the buyers began to grin maliciously. *Lao* Tao and *Lao* Chong's faces blanched. *Lao* Syy nervously pulled back the bolt of his carbine one more time. A .30 caliber bullet the size of his little finger sprung out, and another bullet automatically sprang in to place. The copper cartridge glistened as it landed tip–down in a clump of grass beside him. All rifles in the jungle were trained straight towards the group of buyers.

Lao Tao and *Lao* Chong simultaneously gave out the cry and dove into the underbrush, heading for their village. The five or six buyers wearing the khaki–colored uniforms of policemen raced after them. Abruptly rounds of gunfire exploded. The men in the khaki–colored uniforms were mowed to the ground, blood spurting. The openback pick–up revved up as if to speed down the mountainside, but crashed full–speed into a tree on the side of the road and came to an abrupt halt. Bits and pieces of the truck sprayed into the air in all directions from the impact of the bullets. Thin–trunked trees were mowed down and folded over on themselves from the force of bullets fired from guns of every description. The frenzied gunfire continued to sound out and the stench of the gun smoke burnt at the nostrils.

"*Kao Ying*! Victory!" someone cried out, the cry competing with the gun-shots. The gun fire slowly subsided into silence. Then the cheers of many men rose louder and louder, almost in unison, except for *Lao Syy*, who whispered softly, "Victory? But these thieves will be remembered as valiant men."

The Necklace

This year's April sun was hotter than any before. It appeared to be scorching everything, desiccating all in view. Leaves, if not parched to a red-brown color, had wilted to faded green and looked like they would soon die. The breeze blew intermittently, but only to sweep the burning heat against one's skin. The land in the vicinity of this village still had no trees tall enough to help block the sun's rays or the hot wind. By the time they moved down to these mountain foothills less than three years ago, all the big trees in the forest had already been uprooted by gigantic machinery.

Lao Jong walked over to the waterstand. He took the water dipper made from a half-gourd and, scooping up some cloudy white water from the clay jar, drank it thirstily. The tea he had boiled earlier had already vanished from the jar.* Today he was drinking more water than any other day. He gazed absently at the public well far in the distance. Its water was also almost gone. The sun's rays danced and shimmered, keeping time with the noisy chirping of the cicadas that were all about. Everything was so dry. The only exception was the mountain range on the horizon, its blue-green majestically peaceful and coolly refreshing.

This year was exceptionally arid. Two or three days ago his friends who had just come down from Mount Intanon† told him that it was also dry in the mountains. It was especially bad where the military superhighway was starting to erode. Most of the trees in that area were pitifully desiccated. The famous Delavayi Rhododendron trees and sphagnum mosses that the city folk like to

---

*Unlike lowland village Thai who drink well or rain water, many hilltribe groups such as the Hmong drink boiled tea.

†Mount Intanon, located in Chiang Mai province, is Thailand's highest mountain. An important military communications installation was built at its peak, and a military road constructed to reach it. Various hilltribe groups, including Hmong (or Meo, as they are also called), live here and throughout the mountain ranges in northern Thailand. These ethnic minority groups generally practice "swidden" or shifting agriculture, in which forest plots are cleared and planted for a few years and then allowed to revert to nature.

come up to admire already looked dead.* And it wasn't at all clear if they would revive enough in the upcoming rainy season to bloom, as they usually did, in the cold season.

He had also heard that lowlanders both near and far away were complaining that there was not enough water for them to plant in the dry season. The irrigation canals weren't carrying as much water as in previous years. But *Lao* Jong was neither happy nor sad about this news because neither he nor his fellow villagers planted or planned to plant in the dry season anyway.

"Let's go. Are you ready to go yet?" *Ee* Moi, his wife, reproached him. He returned the gourd water dipper to its rest. He turned and grabbed his machete laying nearby.

"Okay. Let's go. We should try to hurry. There are only two of us to do the work. Otherwise we will be behind everyone else, just like last year," he replied gently as he opened the door and walked out in front. Extending him a banana-leaf cigar, *Ee* Moi followed him.

Their black clothes really absorbed the heat. After just moments in the sun, their clothes pressing against their skin felt as if they would catch fire any minute, were it not for their pouring sweat to douse it. The trees and branches that the two of them had cut and stacked on a previous day were now dry and brittle in the middle of the sunshine. *Lao* Jong inhaled the cigar smoke before he spoke, without turning around to look at his wife.

"Look, with such strong sunshine, everything really dried quickly. I'm worried that the people around us will burn their fields before us. Once they start burning, their fire will spill over to our fields, just like last year. It will burn what we have cut before we have a chance to collect the firewood. And we'll have problems with the trees we haven't felled yet because the fire will burn the surrounding kindling. If we burn after everyone, there won't be enough kindling left to finish burning off the weeds. Lowlanders don't know how to do upland agriculture properly. When they decide they want to burn, they just do so. Once they've started their fires, they don't pay much attention to the other uses the fields could have. They don't want to ask us how to do it properly because they are afraid of loosing face to mountain people."

"Of course. We've been so slow," *Ee* Moi replied to her husband's lament. "You lost so much time waiting to hire a tractor. When that wasn't possible,

---

*Because of its unique ecology, Mount Intanon is the only place where the Delavayi Rhododendron (*kulaap phan pii*) grows in Thailand. Reaching 4-12 meters high, these trees are famous for their stunningly beautiful clusters of red flowers which bloom beginning in February. Found together with the rare sphagnum moss (*khaotok ryysii*), both plants grow in densely forested pockets at high altitudes where it is cool and there is abundant moisture.

that left just the two of us to do all the work by ourselves. So how could we possibly keep up with them?"

Lao Jong felt a flash of anger. He glanced briefly at his wife's face. As he turned away, he teased her gently, "Precisely, how much can two people do? I'd like to find another wife or two, so there would be three or four of us to do the work."

"If you have the money to marry more, go ahead. Then things will be easier for me. I'll have someone to help me work in the fields," *Ee* Moi retorted instantly.

Soon the two reached the area where they had left off in the morning. Diverse scents from the trees and branches that had been cut and stacked into piles wafted to their noses. The leaves had curled into gray-green tubes from the heat of the sun.

Husband and wife extinguished their banana-leaf cigars and put them away for later. They began to cut the remaining trees with expert skill. Soon the patch of forest would be flattened to the ground. From nearby fields, the sound of the tractors roared up from time to time. Each time the roars completely drowned the sound of their two machetes hitting the trees.

"With only five *rai* of land, if we leave the tree stumps in the ground as we did when we farmed in the mountains, what can we plant to support us? Especially these days, when the prices for crops are so low," *Lao* Jong complained as he raised his shirtsleeve to wipe off the sweat dripping into his eyes. He looked over towards his wife who was absorbed in slashing the trees. She stopped abruptly and looked at her husband quizzically before answering.

"If we don't leave the stumps, we would have to bend way over low to the ground to fell them. Why would we do that? The lowlanders don't know how to cut trees efficiently at all. They cut low down to the ground. That way really hurts the back. Even leaving stumps one or two feet off the ground hurts badly enough as it is."

"No, no. I don't mean that. Of course leaving taller stumps is better. Not only is it easier on the back, but it has the advantage that next year it will have branches and leaves that we can use to burn off the weeds again. But here is not like in the mountains where we can clear as much land as we want. On a small plot of land like this, planting just between the stumps like we did in the mountains means we won't be able to plant enough to eat." *Lao* Jong stopped speaking briefly and glanced at his wife. Seeing she was still listening intently, he continued speaking as he cut the trees before him.

"That's why I wanted to hire a tractor to dig out the tree stumps. We'd just have to hire it one time and we would be fine. But we have no money."

Ee Moi appeared angry. "When will you quit talking about the tractor for once and for all? Last year you were obsessed with waiting for the tractor and

so we fell behind everyone else. Why are you so focussed on it? Each of our
two hands are still strong. Once we have burned off the fields, we can help each
other dig and pull out the tree stumps. Soon it will be done. Do you want to
sell another necklace?"

Lao Jong was speechless. He tried to swallow the pain deep in his breast.
His left hand unconsciously reached up and touched the silver necklace at the
base of his throat. His largest and most beautiful necklace was no longer there.

He thought back to when he had first come down from the mountains.
He didn't blame himself for moving because he had been taken in by the radio
advertisement broadcast in his language. Things had come to the point that he
and his friends had to resettle because there was no viable land left near their
old village for cutting and clearing upland fields. The land was all degraded.
The good land near their village for planting upland crops throughout their
lifetimes had become private property. Some of his friends resettled higher on
the mountains not far from their old places, but he, *Ee* Moi and a few friends
chose to settle in the lowlands both out of curiosity and the dream that maybe
it would be as good as the radio claimed.

When they first came down from the mountains, he felt excited and proud
that everyone welcomed him and his friends so warmly. The district officer
thanked them all for cooperating with the government by not planting opium
and cutting down the forest. He and his friends received prepared house plots
without any of the complications that many lowlanders faced. When *Ee* Moi
told the doctor that she didn't want to have any children yet because she still
had to help her husband farming, the doctor gave her a free injection and told
her at the same time that if after one year she still didn't want to have any children, she should come again for another injection. And if she developed any
abnormalities of her uterus, the doctor would treat her for free. A group of
well-dressed Caucasians and Thais came to their homes and introduced them
to a new religion.* This religion had only one spirit, who was very powerful.
Any given year one only had to host one or two ceremonies. It didn't require
any elaborate ritual offerings. It didn't have to be fed often or given very much,
unlike the mountain spirits. And those who worshipped this single spirit
helped each other out all the time. Eventually, *Lao* Jong and his group decided to convert and worship this single spirit.

"These thorny bushes don't need to be cut. They're already dry and there
is a lot of cogon grass around here. Once we start the burn, they will catch fire
easily." *Ee* Moi said, interrupting his thoughts.

---

*Christian missionaries have been active among the Hmong.

In the end the trees in the area were all felled. Only scattered stumps and thorny bushes remained. The neighboring plots of land had long been cleared by the power of labor and the ever-transcendent power of money. The sun was setting behind the mountaintops, spreading its golden glow over the landscape.

"Moi, why don't you go back to the housework. I can collect the firewood by myself," he said to his wife. She was resting, smoking a cigar on a nearby hillock. With no further ado, she got up and started to walk off. She turned around to tell *Lao* Jong,

"Don't come back too late, okay? Don't worry if you can't get it all done. Tomorrow we will help each other collect fire wood all day and it will be fine. The day after that we can help each other prepare the firetrails. And then all that is left is the burning itself."

Lao Jong nodded his head in agreement, but he continued sitting smoking his cigar. He let his thoughts wander. After the burning, they would still have to hoe and loosen the soil. They couldn't afford to wait for rain to soften the earth first. They probably didn't have enough time to dig out the tree stumps. Otherwise it would be like last year all over again. If they planted after everyone else, they might as well not plant at all. He vividly recalled last year's painful lesson.

Last year he planted sweet corn for a foreign-owned canning factory just like the majority of the other villagers in his village. Corn is easily planted; its roots are like those of opium poppies and he had planted it before. Villagers who encouraged him to plant it told him that it was easier than other crops because one didn't have to invest capital and didn't have to take much risk. The factory would loan them the seeds, fertilizer, and pesticides. At harvest, the company would buy the whole crop at a guaranteed price of one baht per kilo. Furthermore, if they had a good crop, the company wouldn't charge for the seeds they borrowed.

Lao Jong thought scornfully of those who had encouraged him to join and spoken as if the factory's system was the best way in the world to help the farmers. In fact, if those villagers knew about the way opium was planted in the mountains, they would be ashamed of themselves. In the mountains, people who plant opium can even ask their buyers for cash advances equal to the value of their entire opium crop. In addition, they don't have to bother with signing any confusing papers. Furthermore, the harvest price per *rai* was much higher. And what's more, if one borrowed money and had a bad harvest, one could postpone the loan and pay it back in the following year without even having to pay interest.

Thinking about investment capital upset him even more since it was the reason that everything went wrong last year. He had waited and waited for the loan he thought he could get from the cooperative to hire a tractor. By the time he was certain that he wouldn't get any money, it was almost too late to plant. He and his wife had only been able to do a superficial job of felling the trees as they rushed to get the fields planted. Even though his friends who had already finished their fields came to help, he still finished planting his fields a week later than everyone else. So of course his sweet corn matured later than everyone else's. When the company's truck came to buy the crops, he was not ready to sell. He had to plead for the factory's truck to come back for his on a different day. Perhaps because his corn crop was small, they weren't very interested in it, but the company didn't come until several days after the appointed time. By that point, most of his corn crop was too ripe for canning standards. He almost had to beg the company people to buy his crop, even though they offered a price lower than originally guaranteed. The company representatives kindly agreed to help him out by buying just enough of his crop so that he could pay back the cost of the seed, fertilizer and insecticide. For months, he and his wife had to eat boiled corn instead of rice.

He threw away the banana leaf cigar stub that had gone out by itself in his hand. He got up, chose wood that was big enough to use as firewood and collected it into piles. As he bent and stooped gathering the wood, the two silver necklaces around his throat knocked against each other making a clinking sound. The sound reminded him of their presence and of the loss of his largest and most beautiful necklace, the one which had the most meaning for him and which never should have escaped him.

It had happened because he had been open to new experiences. With everyone singing the praises of cooperatives, *Lao* Jong had been thoroughly convinced and asked to join the subdistrict cooperative immediately. When he needed 70 baht as the initial registration fee, he didn't hesitate to remove his necklace and pawn it with a merchant in the town market. Once he received the loan from the cooperative, he planned to redeem it.

He couldn't remember how many times he had walked to ask about the loan from the cooperative. Each time took at least half a day. The answer he would get was "we don't have the money yet," "the money hasn't come yet," and finally "the money came, but it was not enough." The last answer made him despair. The government didn't have enough money, but without sufficient funds how was it supposed to help anyone? After that, his necklace fell into the hands of the pawnbroker, but not until after he walked back and forth to pay the interest of 14 baht per month for almost 10 months. And it was a thousand times more painful when he finally realized that the "credit" of hilltribe people like him was not considered good enough for them to be able to borrow money easily. Even if the cooperative had money, they didn't want ·to lend it to him. He had no assets to use as collateral. Although he had land, that was meaningless since it had no legal title. It was as if lowlanders only trusted what was on "paper."

Ee Moi had cried when she learned about it. It would have been better to have lost his two smaller necklaces than to have forfeited the big one. But how could anyone have known that he would have to lose it? That large necklace was the reason that he and *Ee* Moi met and eventually married.

Five years ago, at the *nohbaejo* festival celebrated in the mountain village, the boys and girls had had a good time playing *bohkohnnaa* with each other.* The boys always lost this ball game. Then the girls were able to confiscate their necklaces. According to custom, they forced the youth to ransom them back, some with songs, some by dancing, and others by blowing the *tamyia* and *kaeng* musical instruments until the girls were satisfied. His large necklace was confiscated by *Ee* Moi. She wouldn't return it until he won it back playing *bohkohnnaa*. She felt that the boys had lost too easily and she acted as if she was going to quit playing.

He lifted the pile of firewood onto his shoulders and prepared to return. These five *rai* of land stretched far enough to make him feel alone and separate from other villagers who were working their own plots. But the fact that he was a hilltribesman, a mountain person, already made him feel like a stranger in this village. As a result of the land lottery, he received a plot next to lowlanders who were not very friendly towards him.

The rays of the sun had long disappeared, but it was not yet completely dark. He threw the pile of firewood that he had been carrying in the yard by his house. He stopped for a moment and stood with his head bowed looking intently at the ground. If only the farming plots had been plowed like the land around his house, it would be wonderful. Sighing as he thought about it, he opened the door to his hut and went inside. *Ee* Moi greeted him the moment she saw him.

"You're home earlier than other days. Is something wrong? You look worried."

"Never mind. I've just been doing too much thinking. Is there something you want me to help you with?"

"No, nothing. Everything's ready. We could eat right away, but if you want to rest first that's fine too."

---

* *Nohbaejo* festival is a New Year festival celebrated annually in January. One of the key events is the ball-throwing, or *bohkohnnaa*, in which young men and women line up opposite each other and throw a cloth ball back and forth. Whenever someone drops the ball, deliberately or not, they must pay a forfeiture.

Lao Jong didn't say anything. He collapsed and sat down on the ground in his house near the hearth. *Ee* Moi handed him a stool, but he didn't take it. He preferred to sit on the ground. In his house only the sleeping platform and kitchen shelf were not flush on the ground. Old memories returned. The song that *Ee* Moi sang after he ransomed the necklace when he won the *bohkohnnaa* game echoed in his mind.

Jyy lang to dae yyy juu, tyyn tuu tae yaakaa mua tuu mua trong.
Jae saa tyy trong plaaj jia wong kuu mua jao jia tia kua am plaa.

Just as creeks flow in their beds,
so brides pass through the doors of their homes
to live with their husbands like penned pets.
The girls' tears flow with the suffering welling in their hearts.

He took the teacup from his wife that she had poured for him, and his thoughts became even more disquieted. He didn't want to think that he was the cause that his beloved wife must suffer. As a husband he tried to help his wife far more than other men in the mountains. Hilltribe men assumed the responsibilities for hosting visitors and engaging in business trade, but they left their wives and children to do the farming. Those with money took on several wives to help with the farm work. But *Lao* Jong tried to work the fields even more than his wife. And no matter how much money he had, he didn't think about taking other women as wives.

Lao Jong picked up a cigar and lit it. He inhaled several times in succession. *Ee* Moi looked at him with strange look in her eyes and smiled at him slightly before speaking.

"Don't worry so much. I have thought it through. I will give you my necklace and bracelet to sell and we will have enough money to hire a tractor. Even if we can't plow it all, it will still help a lot. If we get a good price for our crops this year, you can buy me new ones. Otherwise, it's alright if you can't. I will wear just one necklace to make sure that the spirit *tuchengtuchii* in our old village will recognize me, that's enough."

Lao Jong looked at his wife. When he saw how earnest her eyes were, he was shocked. "What are you saying? There is no way I will do that. I have already lost one and that pains me greatly. Are you sure that if we sell yours, we will have enough money to buy it back? I have already been hurt enough by the cooperative. Don't let yourself be hurt by the company too. I won't do that. I certainly won't let you suffer like that."

Ee Moi avoided his eyes and asked as casually as possible, "And so what will you do?"

Lao Jong clenched his teeth so hard his cheeks bulged for a time, before he answered tensely, "We will do as much as we can. Let's see how things go this year. If nothing improves, I will take you back home to the mountains."

As he was speaking, he poured the tea into the ashes of the fireplace. The smell of the charcoal ash as the water hit it rose up and filled his nostrils. It was like the smell of the fields as they soaked up the first rain after they were burned. It was a smell that was buried in his blood since the days of his ancestors. It was a smell that gave new hope of a new prosperity taking root. When he lived in the mountains, this was the smell that permeated the air throughout the whole village at the beginning of the rainy season. It was the sign that everyone had aged another crop, another year.

"Water belongs to the fish.
The sky belongs to the birds.
The mountains belong to the Meo."*

Ee Moi murmured the saying disconsolately in the language of the central Thai. The husband and wife fell silent. Tears welled in their eyes.

---

* A famous Thai saying. Central Thai is the official language of the Thai government. In addition to their own language, Hmong living in the northern provinces of Thailand are more likely to speak the northern dialect of Thai rather than central Thai.

Glossary

Ai

or

Term of address for fellow villager older in age than the speaker. If used with someone not known for a long time not on close terms, the word becomes extremely rude.

Chawnaaj

Overlord or boss. Used by villagers to address or refer to government officials, particularly policemen, or others in positions of authority.

Ee

Used before the names of females who are younger or equal in age, with whom the speaker has close relations. Used otherwise, the term becomes rude.

Kamnan

Head of a sub–district (tambon) comprised of many villages. Also a village headman of a village within the tambon, generally elected from among the wealthiest members of the community.

Lung

Uncle. Used as term of address for any older, middle–aged villager.

Mae Thao

"Old mother"; grandmother. Used to indicate respect when speaking to elderly village women.

Maekhaa

Vendor.

Maenaaj

Term of address used by employees to female employer. "Mae" literally means "mother," and "naaj" means "master" or "mistress."

Miang

Fermented tea–leaf eaten with salt or ginger.

Paa

Aunt. Used as term of address for any older village woman.

Baht

Unit of Thai currency equal to approximately one U.S. dollar in 19.

Phaasin	Long–length skirt worn by village women.
Phaakhaomaa	Piece of woven cloth used by village males. May be used as turban, tied; around waist as belt, worn as informal sarong, or used in numerous other ways.
Phii	Older sister or older brother. Used as term of address for someone slightly older than the speaker with whom speaker has close relationship. Also used by wife in speaking with or to her husband.
Phiichaaj	Older brother. Used as polite, but informal, term of address for male older than speaker, but whom speaker does not know well.
Pho Liang	Term of respect usually used by person of little social standing to address wealthy, influential person, especially if one has or is about to receive particular favor.
Rai	Unit of land approximately equal to 0.4 acres or 1,600 square meters. One rai yields an average of 30–60 thang of rice per season.
Salyng	Unit of Thai currency equal to 25 satang or one baht; one–quarter of a baht.
Satang	Unit of Thai currency; 100 satang equal one baht.
Sork	Length equivalent to distance between tip of hand and elbow; equivalent to 50 centimeters.
Thang	Measure equal to 20 liters of rice, about 10 kilograms.
Yai	Grandmother. Used as term of address for elderly woman. May denote an older middle–aged woman with whom speaker has no close bond.

Credits

"A Curse on Your Paddyfields" was originally Published in *Jaturat* 1, No. 20 (25 November 1975):48-9.

"Daughter for Sale" was originally published in *Jaturat* 1, No. 23 (16 December 1975):50-51.

"Escaping the Middleman" was originally published in *Jaturat* 2, No. 27 (13 January 1976):40-41.

"Bitterness and the Sold Water Buffalo" was originally published in *Jaturat* 2, No. 35 (9 March 1976):42-3.

"Dividing the Rice" was originally published in *Jaturat* 2, No. 31 (10 February 1976):44-45.

"The Fount of Compassion" was originally published in *Jaturat* 2, No. 34 (2 March 1976):42-3.

"Burmese Buddha Images" was originally published in *Jaturat* 2 No. 65 (5 October 1976):48-9.

"Amphorn's New Hope" was originally published in *Jaturat* 2, No 43 (4 May 1976):36-37.

"Khunthong's Tomorrow" was previously unpublished; written in August 1976.

"Rit's First Mistake" was written in March 1978; translation made from this manuscript version. It was published in 1979 in a collection of short stores titled *Khlyan Hua Daeng*, edited by Suchart Sawatsri (Bangkok: Duang Kamol).

"Before Dawn" was written in 1976; previously unpublished.

"Kao Ying!" was originally published in *Jaturat* 2, No.59 (24 August 1976):48-9.

"The Necklace" was published in an anthology of contemporary short stories edited by Suchart Sawatsri under the title *Raakhaa Haeng Chiwit* [The Price of Life], 1979.

Center for Southeast Asian Studies
University of Wisconsin-Madison
Monograph Series

Voices from the Thai Countryside: "The Necklace" and Other Stories
by Samruam Singh, edited and translated by Katherine Bowie

Population and History: The Demographic Origins of the Modern Philippines
edited by Daniel Doeppers and Peter Xenos

Sitti Djoaoerah: A Novel of Colonial Indonesia
by M. J. Soetan Hasondoetan, translated by Susan Rodgers

Face of Empire: United States - Philippines Relations, 1898-1946
by Frank Hindman Golay

Inventing a Hero: The Posthumous Re-Creation of Andres Bonifacio
by Glenn May

The Mekong Delta: Ecology, Economy, and Revolution, 1860-1960
by Pierre Brocheux

Autonomous Histories, Particular Truths: Essays in Honor of John Smail
edited by Laurie J. Sears

An Anarchy of Families: State and Family in the Philippines
edited by Alfred W. McCoy

Salome: A Filipino Filmscript by Ricardo Lee
translated by Rofel Brion

Recalling the Revolution: Memoirs of a Filipino General
by Santiago Alvarez, translated by Paula Carolina S Malay

Anthropology Goes to War: Professional Ethics and Counterinsurgency in Thailand
by Eric Wakin

Putu Wijaya in Performance: An Approach to Indonesian Theatre
edited by Ellen Rafferty

Gender, Power, and the Construction of the Moral Order
edited by Nancy Eberhardt

A Complete Account of the Peasant Uprising in the Central Region
by Phan Chu Trinh, translated by Peter Baugher and Vu Ngo Chieu